Do not find me

Do not find me

KATHLEEN NOVAK

THE PERMANENT PRESS
Sag Harbor, NY 11963

For information, address:
The Permanent Press
4170 Noyac Road
Sag Harbor, NY 11963
www.thepermanentpress.com

Library of Congress Cataloging-in-Publication Data

Novak, Kathleen—
    Do not find me / Kathleen Novak.
        pages ; cm
    ISBN 978-1-57962-427-9
        1. Fathers and daughters—Fiction. 2. Family secrets—
Fiction. 3. Minnesota—Fiction. 4. New York (N. Y.)—Fiction.
5. Psychological fiction. 6. Mystery fiction. I. Title.

PS3614.O9265D6 2016
813'.6—dc23   2015042064

Printed in the United States of America

for my family

*T*he old fishermen pitched a chisel three feet in front of them before they took a step onto the ice. That's how they measured the safety level, the depth, the sureness with which they could proceed. My father fished that way all his life. He took me out when I could only toddle along holding to the back hem of his parka. "Pay attention," he'd call over his shoulder to me, to himself, maybe even to the schools of walleye and crappie swarming beneath the ice layer. Life is perilous for all creatures. That's what the fishermen knew. They knew to pitch the chisel ahead of them before they stepped out onto the ice.

ONE

November 15, 2011

My father died last week, leaving me his small house on the lake, his whole shed of tools, his sparse belongings. "Meggie, just toss a match to the lot," he'd said. "But not my tools." Then he'd smiled in his faraway manner, only partially available, the bobber tipping about cheerfully, while the bait hung deep below. "Pay attention." He knew that most dangers are not so readily seen, that most dangers remained keenly below the surface, in the darker waters, in the soul's long night. As a fisherman he knew that.

When you are an only child and your mother dies early, you cling to what is left. My mother named me Margaret after her mother who died young of a ruptured aneurysm, just as my own mother did. I came home from a normal day of fifth grade spelling, math, and safety patrol to find my mother lying on the kitchen floor, the egg beater resting on her opened fingers and the whipping cream still liquid in its bowl on the counter. I screamed until I found my good common sense. Then I called my father at the jewelry store, pictured him reaching across his long table of tools and broken trinkets, pushing his goggles onto his head to pick up the phone, through which I would tell him his wife of fifteen years was no more.

A whole year went by before I remembered anything. My father, however, acted swiftly on my behalf. He brought in one of his sisters to help with dinners and laundry and the general order that had been my mother's specialty in life. Our routines continued. But what did not continue, what my Aunt Natty could not sustain, was the fact of a mother. I no longer had a mother like every other girl I knew. My friend Ellie back then had divorced parents, but she lived with her mother. My friend Michelle's mother worked where she had to travel almost half the time, leaving her daughter to cook the dinner and help get her siblings to bed, which we all thought truly outrageous. But at the end of the week Michelle's mother returned with small shampoos and soaps from the hotels and motels where she had stayed. Mothers do things like that. They search the landscape for loose bits they can bring back to the nest. At some fundamental level a mother is always a mother. Nobody else fulfills that particular role, not even a father.

My father at least wanted to keep me company. He tried. In spite of the underlying distraction that seemed to encompass my father, he tried to be present, he tried to teach me and stay in my world. He'd grown up in the town where I grew up, but as a young man he'd gone to New York. He'd repaired jewelry on Madison Avenue for several years and then returned here. He was hired by the best jeweler in town, and he met and married my mother. Five years later I was born. In all my life I could not entice my father to go to New York with me. "I want to see where you worked and the the-aters where Aunt Bella sang and Little Italy and ride the subway and eat a hot dog on the street." I begged him forever. New York was the center of civilization to me, and my own father had lived there just at the time when Bob Dylan rose to fame and Woody Allen. My father had rolled into town just as the town began to roll into a new era. He didn't return, and he never indulged my New York fantasies. He remained as solid as he knew how to be. And that's how my childhood went, motherless but steady.

I have so much on my mind now, left as I am, holding the bag. His possessions, his last week, the memories of him and, now that he is gone, the memories of my mother as well. For ten years I had a mother and father. Then for thirty-two years I had only my father. Now for the rest of my life I will have a mother and father who died. I wonder if that makes sense to anyone else. They are together again in their absence. So when I look at this small house that he moved to years after I left, I see the soap he bought at the dollar store the last time he was well enough to shop in town, and I see that the soap is in a dish that was part of my mother's original set, a perfectly white dish decorated in many colored flowers with tiny leafy vines. I find them together everywhere. A week ago, when my father still lived, I saw only him in this house, his worn furniture, the pillows propping him in his bed, his small repair tools laid out precisely on a bench, his heavy old boots at the door.

But now I see how my mother's matching chairs, upholstered in gray tweed the month before she died, sit at angles, close to the wood-burning stove with all my father's fire-tending tools. Her dish towels, embroidered with each day of the week enacted by a different cute kitten, hang on the rack by the sink along with my father's crinkled leather mitts, left there probably weeks ago to dry from some outdoor task. In a high school art class my mother had ventured out with acrylic paints to depict the moon over a still lake. I saw it on the wall over my parents' bed when I was a girl, as I see it now over the bed where my father died last week. So here they are, together in these ways.

I don't live in Northern Minnesota anymore. I moved to the city to go to college and stayed. I got married young, reaching for a whole family again, I suppose. I had two boys before I was twenty-eight. We named one Anthony or Tony, after the Italian grandfather I never knew, and the other Michael or Mickey, after my husband's Irish grandfather, whom he never knew. My boys are in high school now, making their own stories. Until my father got sick, they remained the ultimate center of my universe. I'm still married to their father, but I don't believe he loves me the way he once did, if in fact he ever did really. He's preoccupied with the rest of his life, his high level job, his triathlon training, his poker night, his sons. He's pleasant to me, which is almost more shocking than if he were not. I was not prepared to live in the absence of feeling. It is as though the lake out there could buoy me up without my swimming or floating or clinging to a branch. In my marriage I drift on the surface. I do not sink. I do not go in any particular direction. It's all quite easy. And as long as there are people in the world who love me, I can continue to float this way, I suppose. I look at the sky and often it is strikingly bright blue.

But now I've lost my father. My sons are home studying for tests, training for basketball season, falling in love with pretty girls who want boyfriends. They text me off and on all day, detached little messages that remind me of a life still waiting for me there. Yet I am here. Yesterday and the day before I cleaned out the kitchen, tossing things into boxes and bags with hardly a thought—keep, give away, throw away. I keep my father's knives, which though inexpensive, are all as sharp as a downtown chef's. My father was proud of his tools, tools of every kind, they mattered to him. I keep one cast-iron skillet that he used all his life to fry us eggs or thin, cheap steaks or chunky potatoes smothered in oil. I keep the local phone book and all the notes he'd scribbled in it over the past year, whatever they mean. I put his ChapStick in my purse. I plan to give away every other battered, but reasonably useful thing, the two-slot GE toaster, the dented teapot, even the stainless silver he bought discontinued at the jewelry store when he and my mother were first married, half the pieces bent out of shape or missing. You might think I'd keep them for sentimental reasons. But I don't need them and, ultimately, would never use them. I'm being stern on these matters. If and when you face this same task, I assure you, your sentiments will not rule you. Overwhelmed as I am, you will glance at the clock and the room empty of any worker but yourself, and you will get busy with your head squarely on your shoulders. See if I am not right.

One evening the long summer after my mother died, I waited until Aunt Natty left for the day, then sat on the floor next to my father's chair. "I miss Mama," I said, stating the obvious, perhaps, but still saying something I had not said to him before. He nodded. "Don't you miss her too?" I wanted him to sink into himself, weep, hold me close in our mutual anguish. But he did not. With his elegant hands he smoothed the arm of the chair, again and again, as if it were an animal's wet head that needed such taming, such gentle assuring. He nodded again. "Meggie, your mother filled the house. You and I, Meggie, what are we going to do to fill this house again?"

My ten-year-old self considered this question with utmost resolution. I wasn't sure that the house really did feel empty. I certainly felt empty. Lost, actually. I felt lost in exactly the way I learned the meaning of the word. My path had become so overgrown as to be unrecognizable, so that every step I took involved concentration. I didn't know my direction, I couldn't feel firm dirt when I stepped, I heard strange sounds ahead, and I could not see where I was going. That's how lost I was.

When my father asked about filling the house, I said, "Maybe we need a smaller house." This made him laugh, a laugh so hearty and relieved, I laughed too.

"Do you want cocoa?" His eyebrows raised high his invitation.

"In July?" We pulled each other up and went into the kitchen. We made cocoa and floated marshmallows in our cups. While we drank, he told me a story about Aunt Natty trying to woo her high school boyfriend with three-layer cakes. My father's childhood was largely defined by the troupe of older sisters who marched ahead of him—singing songs, making dresses, baking, dreaming, and entertaining the various boys who caught their fancies. Aunt Natty's real name was Natalina. She was ten years older than my father, so when she was scheming her most alluring cakes, he sat on the edge of a kitchen chair transfixed by the layers of cake held together by sugary frosting, a boy of only six or seven. He watched her smooth the frosting along the sides and pile it high on top. "Natty could turn a plain cake into the feathery top of heaven, Meggie. Who could resist?"

"Did the high school boy fall in love with her?"

My father squinted back those thirty some years gone by to who he used to be and what he saw sitting at the kitchen table, his skinny legs wound around and tucked under. Then he grinned at me. "I think he must have. He must have been crazy about her."

"But you don't know, you don't remember?"

"I remember the cakes," he answered.

"So was it Uncle Bill?" I wanted the full story, some story to roll around in my mind and give me even a small path of clarity that lost summer without my mother. "Did she bake the cakes for Uncle Bill?"

Now my father looked a little lost too. Was it Bill back then? Silent, grumpy Bill? He shook his head. "No, Bill came along later, after Natty's true love went down with his plane over Germany. That was Mario. Mario went down and Bill came along to heal the wounds. Big old Bill. Maybe she made cakes for him too. You should ask her."

My Aunt Natty and Uncle Bill never had children, and nobody ever said why. She loved me greatly in her organized way that was much like my mother, efficient and predictable. But I wasn't all Natty's to love, that was the thing. I was my mother's to love and she had died. And Natty had never developed the kind of whole open heart that I think mothers have, that I think I have toward my boys and that my mother had toward me. No, Natty stayed an auntie, a kind and purposeful auntie. And then she too died, in midlife, not many years after my mother. She had a heart condition nobody ever knew about. If she'd experienced sharp pains or short breath, she didn't say. She went along just being Natty, minding her own business, not causing a ripple until it was too late.

The rest of my father's sisters lived or died in other places. Bella, the singer, moved to New York, married a professional waiter, divorced him, married some kind of art dealer, divorced him, and finally settled with an attorney who could manage her interests, or so she said. Years ago, they moved to Manzanillo, Mexico. Throughout my life, I only knew Bella to show up for major events with a heavy, leather-trimmed suitcase holding her perfectly coordinated wardrobe. She was the first one I called to say my father had died.

"My baby brother," she wailed to me. "I've lost him, my Gigi." She cried, while I explained that my father had not told me he was sick until it was too late to help him. He refused doctors, I told her, and made me promise to bury him quickly.

"He didn't want a funeral, Auntie. I'm so sorry. He was so sure about this."

"Oh, of course, of course. Such a private man, who could know. And I'm so far away. Now look. Poor Gigi." She cried a long time on the other end of the line. When her weeping stopped, she said, "What will you do, Margaret dear? Now that you are all alone?" Even her speaking voice is melodic.

"Well, I'm married, you know. I have two sons in high school, so when I'm done cleaning out the house here, I'll go back to my family."

"I suppose," she answered.

"How are you Auntie Bella? How are you feeling?"

"I'm eighty-four now, my dear. So, of course, the sun no longer loves me."

"But are you well? Are you feeling good?"

"Margaret dear, you have no idea. I do not see clearly, of course. I sleep poorly, up at all hours wandering about with these bad eyes, hoping for the moon to guide my way. And then I have to take these pills for blood pressure, as everyone does these days it seems. My hair colorist moved to Mexico City, which has been something else to deal with, as you might imagine."

"But still," I continued, "you're healthy overall. I could visit you sometime soon."

"You're a good girl, Margaret. Gigi raised a lovely daughter, didn't he? Now listen, call me anytime and we'll chat."

"My boys might like a week in Mexico. We could come for a visit," I persisted, suddenly realizing I wanted to see her face, her blue eyes like my father's and her aristocratic chin. She is something of me, so I persisted. "I've actually never been to Mexico, even with all the charter flights and great deals. It would be so nice to see you, Auntie."

"Oh, Margaret," she said in return. "You're such a dear. You have no idea."

My father's oldest sister, Francesca, died during the war. She worked as a Red Cross volunteer and was crushed when a building collapsed during a raid in London. Francesca became the family's saint, the tallest, smartest, most beautiful sister, the one who taught her siblings to read, who rolled her sisters' hair in handmade curlers, and saved the soldiers in war before she died a heroine at age twenty. My father barely knew her. He was only five when she died. But still he talked about her, told the stories that Natty had told him, kept a picture of her wearing her crisp Red Cross uniform in a tiny silver frame. There she is on his dresser, seventy years later, seriously eyeing the camera, ready to move into the world of war and do whatever it needed her to do.

The second oldest sister, my Aunt Mary, got married to her high school sweetheart and moved to Los Angeles so he could make it big in real estate. Maybe he did. Certainly they stayed and made their own life out there in the West. When I was a small girl, Aunt Mary and her husband, Joe, already had grown girls, three of them, marrying and having babies and finding jobs. One of those girls demonstrated in protests against the Vietnam War, I remember, which both my parents found so peculiar. Why would a pretty girl from a reasonable family stomp around the streets carrying signs? Aunt Mary and Uncle Joe didn't travel back home very often. They had discovered a paradise that the rest of the family would not even bother to visit. My grandparents were old country and quiet. To them California remained a rambunctious, unsettled place where houses had no basements and people had no roots.

Aunt Mary still lives in California, an eighty-eight-year-old widow with daughters who are also old. I don't know any of them. They are the fish that got away, I suppose, slipped the hook and never returned to see what they were missing. I called Aunt Mary after talking to Bella. Her voice on the line sounded strong and alert, actually younger than Bella's. All that sunshine maybe. She told me she was sorry. She said she thought her brother was possibly the sweetest man alive. Then she wished me well. I forgot to ask after her daughters. I never sent her a sympathy card when Uncle Joe died, either. It happened the winter my Tony broke his arm trying to ski. That's the fact. But the truth is I'd seen Uncle Joe only once in my life and Mary only twice. I didn't have anything to say.

All my grandparents were gone before I was born, leaving me without the kind of connections that tie decades and generations together, all ages smiling in the family photos, secure in a blood-line that goes on and on, stalwart, even immortal. Not so our family. We have turned out to be so very ephemeral. Maybe Aunt Bella will live on in one of her recordings from the 1960s. She did make numerous recordings. She enjoyed a mild form of immortality all her own. But on the whole, we have not made a long-term showing.

Maybe I should have named one of my boys John or Giovanni after my father, though everyone in his life called him Gigi, a name that can only be his. My father never cared to claim the full Giovanni that was his right; even to himself he remained Gigi. My Tony was about four when he first heard it. "That's a funny name that man called Grampa," Tony whispered in my ear, spraying me with spit and talking so loud everyone in the room could hear him anyway. My father laughed like crazy. He really loved my boys. I think he mostly loved how boy they were, how cocky, male, kick-the-can tough they tried to be. He had never been that way, raised by gentle, foreign parents in a house of girls. Every time one of the boys burped unchecked, my father would absolutely roar. So, of course, they'd do it again.

God, memories can live large. Sometimes larger than the moment we're in. I see my boys sitting at the table trying to make Grampa laugh with their burps, and I don't even see the ForceFlex garbage bags earmarked for the things I will throw away. I don't even see them. But how well I see my father ten years ago, still almost young, sixty-something, with his skin smoothed by wind and sun, a retired jewelry repairman who wanted just then to be in a rough little house on a lake with odd animal cries in the middle of the night and the cycle of water to ice to water as the months moved along.

Mid-November now, the lake has already formed ice, but my father would not have fished it just yet. At a deep level he mistrusted

November weather. Sleet, storms, and high howling winds. Winter pulling time fiercely in its own direction. Every year he reminded me of the *Edmund Fitzgerald* sinking into Lake Superior, its crew playing cards and waiting for the rough waves to diminish, not guessing the storm would turn for the worse and all of them would die, fathers like himself he would say. "That's November, Meggie. Wear your hat and keep your wits about you—it can all change in a minute." Of course, we weren't out in the vast territory of Lake Superior. We were on flat ground in Northern Minnesota, with storm windows in place and a furnace that worked. Nonetheless he found November wily and the ice on lakes in November wily as well. And now he has died in this mistrusted month.

When he lived in town, my father had to pack up to go ice fishing, organizing his tidy trunk with minnows and tackle, his chisel, auger and rods, collapsible stools, and lunch. He tucked a flask of whiskey in his pocket for an extra jolt of warmth and drove to his favorite lake. One year it might be Little Swan. Another year it might be Sand or Buck Lake, Five Island or Pelican. For many years in a row he fished Dewey, a very particular spot on the ice that he came to regard as his own, because the fish found him every time, they returned to him sitting in the cold tending his meticulously cut hole in the ice, almost as though they had a pact to meet in this way, my father with his kindly desire to catch them and the variety of fish looking for food in their cold, solitudinous depths. "You think they'd be onto you by now," I told him one Saturday late in winter when we made yet another visit to his spot on Dewey Lake. "I mean, Dad, this doesn't end well for them."

"They know me," is what he answered. He didn't look at me when he said this, but continued his meditative gaze into the black water. "They know your dad, Meggie."

"Good grief. Then they should know that you're going to yank them out and they'll die. And then you'll eat them." I was about fifteen then, the same age as my Mickey is now. Fifteen-year-olds know pretty much everything. "Fish are dumber than I thought," I concluded. Then we sat on our stools without speaking. Overhead the sky stretched as white as the snow-covered lake. I heard cars out on the county road, a distant hum and a world apart from my father and his fish.

When we drove home in the heated car with a tape of Billie Holiday blasting beautiful misery around us, my father said, "The fish really do know me. Whatever vibrations my breathing makes, the shadow of my body sitting up above them, maybe my voice." He glanced across the front seat at me. "I love the fish is what it comes to. Their place in the scheme. Their mystery down there under the ice. They aren't dumb, like you said. They know me." Then he dug into his jacket pocket for his flask and took a sip.

"Dad, you're driving," I yelled at him.

He grinned at me in response, tucked the flask away, and turned up Billie. I went with him one more Saturday that winter to the exact spot where he again hunched over the ice in solemn silence while fish after fish came to him and quietly died at his hand. The next winter I was sixteen and too busy for ice fishing, but the flow at Dewey Lake had shifted. After two tries, my father moved his meditation to Pelican Lake.

Lost Lake is what I look out at now. Last winter I asked him if the fish were biting. He hated that phrase. "The fish don't bite," he sighed, because after all the years, this was something I should have known, an error in conversation I should not have made. "They come to me," he said.

"So how've they been this year?"

"Pretty good. Lost Lake is still pretty good. A good place for me anyway."

He lived out here fifteen years, and he liked it, I know. Now mid-November maintains without him, the way that places so often outlive us. I've counted nineteen pine trees on this piece of land. My father didn't plant any of them. They greeted him when he arrived, much the same as they waited out his short illness, hung low in his death, and continue to stand guard as I disassemble his house. I look to them every morning. They barely sway in the most harsh November winds, which gives me so much comfort, I can't say.

Even ill, my father's presence filled these rooms and encircled me. He smiled so coherently only an hour before he stopped breathing. I'd made him peppermint tea, which he loved, and handed him a cup on a saucer. He held it delicately and smiled that last smile and gave it back without taking a drop. "All done?" I asked. "All done," he answered, still smiling. Then he closed his eyes as if for a long-needed nap, though of course, he'd been sleeping for most of the week I'd been there. He sighed and fell asleep. And that was his end. Such a nice end, actually. When he was alive and sleeping, I felt less alone than I do at home with everyone off doing their busy lives. When my father was alive, I felt the comfort of being loved. Then he stopped breathing and I was alone. Just that instantly, I was alone. I've heard people say that after a death they felt the loved one nearby, hovering with a palpable energy all around. I felt none of that, none. I sat by him, stroking his arm, watching his face, adjusting the blanket as if it mattered. At dusk I turned the bedside light on, but I didn't move off that chair next to him until an hour later, maybe more. When I stood up to make the phone calls, my whole being ached, a tired and resigned ache that stays with me still.

So I've had these days of being alone. I've taken care of business as survivors must, moving papers and money about, meaningless outward commotion in the midst of something so large as death. I didn't want to look across the desk or counter of these places that require their checks and certificates and signatures. I've thought how my father had to do all this when my mother died, plus work and worry about me. No wonder he asked Natty in. How does anyone navigate the vast geography of death? With a fist of papers? If I were God in heaven, I would laugh until I slipped off my fluffy cloud at the human nonsense of death. Anyway, on my father's behalf, that part is done.

Now also on his behalf, I am sorting the things of his life. I'm doing this alone and in silence, like my father when he fished. I am calm and resolute. Outwardly at least, I show no pain. I do not even want to turn on the radio and hear the peppy announcers bantering about, playing classic hits from the fifties, sixties and seventies, as they say. Elvis followed by Neil Diamond, the Beatles singing "Yesterday." They never play the Rolling Stones or Bob Dylan. If they played Paul Butterfield or Doug Sahm, maybe I'd listen. If they played my father's favorites, Billie, Peggy Lee, Mel Tormé, even Nat King Cole, I'd probably listen. I think they do play Cole's "Lazy-Hazy-Crazy Days of Summer," but my father never cared much for that one anyway. Soda and pretzels and beer had nothing to do with his life. But love did. My father was all about the lyrical lament of love.

"Why do you keep playing this?" I asked him about his obsession with Lena Horne and her "Stormy Weather." *Don't ask why there's no sun up in the sky, stormy weather, since my man and I ain't together, keeps raining all the time.* That was probably when I was in my brilliant fifteenth year again. "Dad, it's summer, the sky is blue. This music is so depressing."

"You're not listening," he said. "You're not paying attention to her voice, Meggie. She tells a whole story in her voice."

I let it go. He'd lost his wife, after all. Before she died my mother told me that my father had come home from New York somewhat broken. She hadn't known him before, but she'd seen him around town. "A looker," she called him, with his lean grace and handsome, almost beautiful face. He was a year older in school, she remembered him, but she hadn't known him. My mother, Miss Carolyn Keene, just like Nancy Drew's pseudonym author, grew up in an apartment downtown with her widowed mother and her brother. After high school she took a few classes in typing and shorthand and got a job working in the office at Bertram's Department Store. She dated some men in town, experienced some failures, learned bridge like so many of her married friends, and had resigned herself to this life when my father walked into Bertram's looking for work.

She recognized him immediately and chatted with him happily while he waited for his interview. That was 1963. He had just come back from New York, well dressed, she told me, so classy she could hardly stand it. She'd actually gone outside herself and asked him to have a cup of coffee with her. After his interview they'd sat side by side at the Woolworth's lunch counter, drinking weak coffee and making friends. "Your father," she said, "was not lighthearted. He was a thinker, a man with many thoughts. And so kind. So kind and good looking."

"So you fell in love with each other?" I asked her, my eight- or nine-year-old self seeking those juicy bits of drama that might make growing up worth the trouble.

"I certainly fell in love with him," she said.

"But didn't he fall in love back? Geez, Mom."

"I know your father loves me, Margaret. That's a lot right there." She patted my knee.

"But he must have proposed to you."

"We went out together. One night we went to a movie, *The Three Stooges Go Around the World in a Daze*. Your father loves that kind of old, slapstick humor. We had so much fun. And he took me to dinner at the hotel one Saturday night. I thought I'd die, I was so proud to be seen with him in his tailored New York suit. He moved so well. You know how he is, anyway. Then the next week President Kennedy was shot. We watched television together in his apartment over the jewelry store there. We watched television and cried. He cried so deeply I thought it would be the end of him. Then it was Thanksgiving and he invited me to Aunt Natty's house. Then Nat said, how great we were together, such a handsome couple." My mother stared off, lost in her mind's eye. "Then we got married right after the New Year. January 4, 1964."

"So he proposed?"

"Something like that," she said.

My mother was twenty-sx when she and my father married and thirty-one when I was born. Her life unfolded in slow motion, which suited her fine, I think. She savored everything—her handsome husband, her little white house on a quiet street near downtown, her baby girl growing day by day, her clean laundry every week and her one cup of coffee brewed fresh each morning. Small details, perfectly executed, delighted my mother. Her life turned when Giovanni Paulo walked into Bertram's that March of 1963. He didn't take the job there. The jewelry store across the street offered him more money. But until I was born, they walked downtown together in the morning and strolled home at five thirty when the stores closed.

"Your father carried a hurt when I met him," she added on that day so long ago, when she told me how he had come into my life. "I know those kinds of things."

"He never said?"

She shook her head. "Maybe he still carries it, when I think about it. But I'm so used to him now. Whatever happened is back then. And he's here now." She patted me again.

After my mother died, my father did not play his music for a while. He'd listen to the radio or keep the television rattling on and on in the living room even when we were not watching it. Billie Holiday and Lena Horne did not speak to a practical wife's death or raising a ten-year-old daughter on your own. I think a year went by, maybe two, before the smoky blues once again wafted through our house.

Maybe because of Billie and Lena, or maybe just because time welcomes the romantic point of view, I find my parents' story of love and marriage backlit and dreamy, while I do not regard my own story that way at all. I see my parents dancing together at the hotel on that night my mother described for me, the smoke-filled room, the dark bar at one end, white linens, the two of them young, attractive, alive. Or I think of them walking home together from their downtown jobs, chatting about the day, the customers who moved in and out of those elegant downtown stores back then, the weather, the easy camaraderie of a young couple with so much before them.

I met my husband at a party in a dumpy apartment near the University of Minnesota. Looking back, I wonder why we all thought those thin-walled, beige-carpeted, crummy buildings were an improvement on the university's dormitories, which at least had reasonably clean hallways and three meals a day. It was a Friday night my senior year. My husband was then a graduate student, a former track star who, nonetheless, knew how to drink his share. He waved at me across the room like we were old friends, like I was supposed to know him. He brought me a rum and Coke without asking. He told me some jokes, I think. His best friend came over to tell me what a great guy I had in my grasp, or some such boy talk that no girl ever falls for anyway. I have to tell my Tony not to brag in this way to impress girls. I don't want to be responsible for adding to their numbers. My Mickey is more like I am, he pulls away, watches, leads with his own uncertainty.

Still I did find my husband funny and smart, interesting overall. We dated until he finished his master's degree and got a job in the management development program at 3M. We got married, but on his territory, not mine. My father came down to the city from Northern Minnesota looking like a duke who had wandered into the commoners' festivities. I don't know why I say that really. It's unfair. But my husband's family lacks a certain refinement. The women fall all over the men, who strut and tease and tell each other how great this is, isn't this the best, that sort of thing. Then imagine my graceful father in one of his dark wool suits, his tie knotted to the fashion, his hair tidy, his fingernails clean and even, everything about him smooth and self-contained. I was so proud of him that day. He walked me down the aisle of some Lutheran church that meant little to either of us and gave me away with his faraway smile.

I didn't marry a man like my father. Clearly I married the first man who cared enough to ask me. I married a man who brought me into his own life, his own enthusiasms and relatives and boring, big church without a thought for what I might really think or want or feel. And in these almost twenty years of marriage, I have yet to remind him. It's my own fault that Billie Holiday sings no songs for me. It's really my own fault.

We are not in accord about my father's death either, my husband and I. Everything that matters to my husband can be measured objectively. If he succeeds at work, then he is promoted or gets a bonus or receives a raise. The impact of his efforts is tangible. This is also true for his triathlon hobby, which is all about times. How long it takes to swim, bike, and run the course. Numbers.

Tangibles. Our home has a specific resale value, our cars a specific devaluation each year. When we added a great room to the back of our house, he calculated the financial benefit, the increased value. For me, the addition provided more space for my boys to play, a lovely view down to the creek, and a massive stone fireplace to set the mood all fall and winter. That's the difference. There's always a difference with us.

My father called to say he was sick on November 1, All Saints' Day. I won holy cards in Sunday school for learning these Catholic holidays. "Meggie," he said, "I've taken a turn here. I cannot seem to eat, keep food down. Maybe you could come up?" He spoke dispassionately, matter-of-fact, can't eat, no food.

"Did you go to the doctor, Dad? Or call?"

"I haven't felt that well, Meggie."

"Tell me your symptoms and I'll call. I'll call the clinic for you."

I waited a long time for him to answer. I stood barefoot in my remodeled great room staring out the wide windows at squirrels dashing madly up and down the backyard trees. I had to some-how save him, my father, call the clinic and corner a doctor who might rush out to my father's bedside and save him.

"Meggie? Maybe you should come up."

I said I would be there by late afternoon, then went into organizing for my trip. I am still my mother's daughter when it comes to efficiency, I'll say that. First, I called my husband to tell him I had to leave for a few days. "Well, get him to a doctor, for heaven's sake," he said. "What's even wrong with him that he can't eat? Too much mercury in the fish up there. Get him a prescription. He'll bounce back."

But when I got here, I knew immediately that whatever was wrong with my father was large and formidable. The boys and I had come to fish with him in early August. Since then, he looked like he'd lost more than thirty pounds, his cheeks hollowed, his wrists all bone, his blue eyes prominent beyond proportion. These normally clean and orderly rooms had not been tended in weeks. "You look pretty sick, Dad," I said as soon as I saw him. "I could call the ambulance. The hospital can get you on an IV, you know, get you some nutrition."

He'd nodded patiently, the way he used to when he was the single father of a preteen with lots of outrageous plans. Parties I might have. A tree house I might build. How we could hitchhike together to San Francisco or buy a motorcycle or paint the house red. "I'm happy here," he said. He smiled. "Thanks for coming." He asked me about the boys and probed for more details, encouraging my stories until, finally, in the middle of one of my elaborations, he fell asleep.

My husband was outraged at me. That I didn't defy my father's backwater notions of health care and call an ambulance, in which case he'd be hooked to a lifeline and on his way to recovery. He ranted for full minutes, and I let him, because I was washing dishes the whole while, accomplishing something that needed to be done, and because the man who loved me best in all of time was in the next room sleeping peacefully with thousands of northern stars winking at him through the bare windows. "Meg, you're being ridiculous," my husband wrapped up in a brilliant finale. "You're just being ridiculous."

"My father knows that he is dying. He wants to stay where he is."

"But what's he dying of? Who dies these days not even knowing? Does he have cancer, are his kidneys failing? What, Meg? It's so ridiculous. Not to even know. My god." Then he lowered his voice. "What are you going to tell Tony and Mick, for god's sake?"

"Right now I'll tell them Grampa is very sick."

"But they'll ask why, Meg. Jesus, you won't listen to reason."

"If they ask why, I'll say he has a serious blockage and cannot eat. I'll tell them he's failing. I'll tell them that all Grampa wants to talk about is them."

"You could still save him."

Then I had to say what I knew was true. "No, I can't."

Over the next few days I kept my family in the city informed of my father's condition. With each passing day he slept more. Otherwise nothing changed that much. Maybe he lost another five pounds before my very eyes, but who would know when he was already so gaunt. He had almost no strength to talk, so he asked questions. He urged me back over old ground—tell him again about my trip to Italy, the long day Tony was born, the third graders I used to teach, my backyard garden. Then he wanted me to tell stories of our years together, Aunt Natty and her meringue pies, school plays, the Christmas tree so huge we couldn't get it through the front door. How I went on and on. Even when he shut his eyes, I kept going just in case he was still awake. I didn't want to let him down.

I called the clinic the first morning after I arrived. A triage nurse informed me that they had no current data for my father. His last physical had been eight years earlier. Back then, at age sixty-seven, he presented no health issues. She reacted with alarm about my father's current symptoms and urged me to get him to a hospital without delay.

"He doesn't want to leave his house," I said.

"I do not recommend it," she replied. After that conversation, I sat down at my father's kitchen table to consider what she would recommend—the ambulance and stark hospital lighting, the impersonal routines, the needles and gauges and tubes. The metal beds and vinyl chairs. Strangers everywhere. Sick people everywhere. Curtains pulled to shut out the day's light and the night's great sky. And would they save him? Could they?

My husband thinks yes. The doctors would have saved him. My ridiculous behavior killed him. Oh, and my father's own ridiculous behavior also killed him. We conspired, my father and I, to let death into this little house, where we generously made it comfortable until it was ready to leave with my father's misguided spirit in tow.

This is a wedge now in our cordial marriage. Aloof as he is, my husband does not like me wandering off into far fields to follow my own primitive notions, or any other kind of notions that do not align with his. This kind of wife does not measure up. His polite calls have come less frequently the longer I am here. You made your choice, his disinterest seems to say, don't expect my sympathy. The boys, though, communicate whenever they have two seconds to text me where they are and what they are doing. So I get the picture of life at home, no matter what my husband does.

The first time I brought my then future husband north, my father still lived in town. We'd driven up in one of those hellish snows that blind all definition of the road and where it is taking you. "What a godforsaken place," my husband remarked as we turned onto the main street, deserted in the early evening cold, snow banks nearing six feet on either side of us. "Who could live up here?" But once inside my father's house, my husband asked eagerly about ice fishing. "So you sit out there all day waiting for fish?" he asked, all hale and hardy, legs crossed, drinking a beer, doing man to man with my father. "So, I mean, what's the technique? One of my college roommates fly-fishes in Wyoming, or Montana, I forget, and it's quite the science. Boxes of flies for different fish, ways to handle the line, snap the wrist. Almost like golf, you know, that kind of precision. Always a technique. Every sport, don't you think?" He had no idea, my future husband, about the kind of man who handles tiny sharp tools to fix the clasp on an intricate pearl necklace handed down through generations, who has known scores of fish to come to him through the darkest waters, and who listens to lonely blues to heal his soul. The kind of man he was roaring along with up in the northland. He had no idea.

My father smiled, as I knew he would. "Ice fishing," he said, "you cut a hole in the ice, and you fish." He nodded once to punctuate what he'd just said.

They did fish together that visit. My father amused, my future husband stunned by the cold and boredom of it all. "We just sat there," he whispered to me as he was taking off his layers of winter clothes. "Just sat on the ice all day like, like stumps."

"Did you catch any fish?" I asked them both.

"Not a bad day," my father called from the bottom of the basement stairs. "Come down here, and I'll show you how to clean them," he said to my future husband, whose jolly notions of being a northern sportsman had already been tested enough. Anyway that's what I remember. My father graciously explaining the fine art of boning and my husband's obvious silence most of that night.

He's not a figment of my mind, this man who pays the bills and plays ball with the boys. He's as real and particular as anyone, I suppose. But because I am so sure I will know his next move, the way he will cross the kitchen to the hall closet before he sets down his work gear, and will only look at us after he's completed this exact task, because he hardly ever surprises me, I can sit here at my father's table and regard my husband as not quite real. As two-dimensional, maybe, or programmed. But that's probably not fair either.

My parents, both buried now, remain real. My sons, my closest friends, the kids I used to teach, all live and breathe and wiggle about in my mind. Why not my husband? When I was a university student, and before I met my husband, I went into a small coffee shop off one of those Paris-like alleyways on a late afternoon, wanting to get some work done before leaving campus. A man sat at a table nearby, engrossed in his papers, tall and thin, impeccable. He wore a camel jacket and a dark turtleneck, tortoise glasses, wool pants. I thought he might be in his midthirties, when men look accomplished and confident, yet are still so vigorous and young. I remember thinking he must be a poet or a professor of poetry. I decided he had shelves of books at home that he'd already read and stacks on his table that he planned to read soon. He'd only fallen in love once or twice, I was sure, with women so deep and dark, not even he could comprehend them. I drank as much coffee as I could hold. I watched him until he put his papers into his leather satchel and left, wanting to follow him, introduce myself, and become one of those deeply mysterious women he loved.

But, of course, I never saw him again. Yet he too remains alive to me. The way his hair waved back just so, as he sat comfortably working at a coffee shop table, not knowing he was becoming some college girl's fantasy. My poor marriage. Here I am envisioning this man in the coffee shop twenty years ago.

Sometimes I think I was able to marry a man like my husband because I had a father who loved me more than anyone else alive. I mean I didn't need unconditional love. I already had it so surely and easily. I'll admit my father was often not fully present. But he was always present when it was important. He'd snap back to me.

When I talked, he barely blinked. He nodded, patted my head or arm, frowned at my difficulties, grinned at my absurdities. So I didn't need to choose a mate who listened to my every word or worried after my every move. Even on my wedding day, I knew my larger love went to my father. My husband got what was left. But here's the thing—that's all he wanted. More devotion would have weighed him down. He's a runner by nature; he travels light.

Now something will change, I suppose. My father is gone and with him the thread to my childhood and how we struggled together when my mother died and the way we shored up in the years later. Now maybe I will need more love somewhere else in my world. After I pack away my father's life here. In a week or two. Even in the midst of my sorting, I cannot believe what it means. That he won't come back and, after a while, neither will I. Still I have this work to do. I must remain focused.

My father kept one tall dresser for as long as I remember. In the bottom drawer, I find his folded sweaters, then T-shirts and sweatshirts in the next drawer up, then pajamas and underwear, socks and scarves and, finally, his jewelry and small mementos in the top drawer. I'm saving all the sweaters and sweatshirts for my boys. Neither of them is conscious of what's in style or not, and they loved their Grampa. As long as they can move freely in their clothes and no other boy has a wise-guy comment, they're good to go with most anything I provide.

The top drawer is my challenge. My father owned two watches he bought used when he worked in New York and restored to a second life. One is a military-issue Timex, the other a gorgeous, heavy Gruen. I try them on and consider the results. I think these old men's watches that my father restored give me a certain dignity. I keep them both on as I continue emptying the drawer, but I am falling in love with the Gruen. It tells perfect time, even now, because my father maintained these watches, whether he wore them or not. He maintained the watches in the same way he maintained his tools. You will not find a dulled scissors or knife, a rusted chisel or wobbly hammer anywhere in my father's world. "Tools let me live," he said years ago, when he was first setting up this house in the woods. He said this as he stood arranging his workshop in the boathouse down by the shore.

"That's a strong comment to make," I'd argued. "I'm sure you could live without them." My father merely raised an eyebrow and kept working.

I've hired a man from town to properly pack my father's tools one more time. My husband will never use these kinds of things, large anvils and tiny, tiny screwdrivers, tweezer-like things of all sizes and knife sharpeners, any number of measuring tools, slides and such, all of them sharp, clean, and maintained.

"You have to watch over things, Meggie," my father told me when I was a girl. "All your life. Whatever it is you love or need or use. Keep things up. Sew on the button, you know? Touch up the paint. Mow your grass."

"Oh, Dad." I shook off that mowing idea.

"Pay attention to what I'm saying, Meggie," was his answer back.

I plan to keep the tools, because I don't really know anyone who will appreciate them, the whole story of what they are and how they served my father's life. My husband has interest in only a few necessary tools, which he insists on purchasing from a prestigious British catalog he discovered online. As if only the British know how to shape a wrench. Whatever. It's a small point. I know he wouldn't want my father's tools and would never use them. But maybe Tony or Mick will grow in that direction. Or maybe I will. I am keeping open to these possibilities. I cannot bear to think that my father's beautiful and valuable tools will not be used again. I'll take them home, just as I'll take home the watches.

"All Swiss parts," my father bragged to me the first time I noticed the Gruen. It was an Easter Sunday somewhere in those teen years, when he wore his best to High Mass at church. "But it was the Gruen family in America that put the watches together. To railroad precision. This watch," he said, holding out his arm for me to see, "this watch could run all the trains in the country. That's perfection." He smiled. "True perfection."

"I never even heard of a Gruen," I believe I muttered.

"That's because the war killed them. Uncle Sam had them building transportation instruments. When customers needed a watch during the war, they had to buy Swiss. After the war they still bought Swiss." He looked at his Gruen. "And that was the end of that story."

These old talks keep rushing in. I can't look forward to new conversations with my father now. I have to hang on to the old ones. So far, there seems no end to them, those random chats throughout my life, bits of advice, explanations, recollections. Meggie this and Meggie that, the name he had for me that no one else used. I am Margaret, after all, as my mother and aunts always called me. My husband says Meg. It's short and modern, I suppose. Margaret is a lot to say and not at all modern. Margaret is the name of a nineteenth-century book heroine, I think. Or someone's elderly aunt. I think that too. But to my father I was Meggie. A sharp pang cuts through me to think I am not Meggie to anyone anymore. Maybe in the future. Maybe I'll introduce myself to a new friend as Meggie. If I can stand it. If that person looks like someone who might love me forever.

My father also kept stacks of evenly folded white handkerchiefs in his top drawer. Alone here in these rustic rooms, he still chose to bleach and iron his handkerchiefs. "Soak the whites," he instructed me the first time I did the laundry by myself. This was at least a year after my mother's death, when Natty had gone home to concentrate on Bill, and my father and I began to truly fend for ourselves. "Put a half cup of bleach in with the detergent and let the clothes soak, Meggie. That's how you get white white." I remember that—white white. I thought to myself then what other kind of white could there be. Now I know, of course. Gray white, yellow white, dirt white. My father's handkerchiefs are, as ever, white white.

Also in the drawer my father chose to put papers that probably had no other home, like his fishing license, his receipt for the rowboat he bought several years ago, a hefty stack of US Savings Bonds secured by a thick red rubber band. I find a key taped to a piece of paper, labeled "motor." I like seeing my father's meticulous printing, both o's perfectly rounded and exact, though I'd forgotten about the motor. Another thing to sell. Now here's Mick texting me about his algebra test. I still have the key in my hand. The key to the motor that propels my father's boat, where my boys love to ride and grin into the backsplash and loll for hours thinking they will catch a fish. Maybe I can't sell this house and property. I look at the box of pans and utensils I've already packed to give away. How long will it take me to put the essential pieces back in their places? What will I need to do to hang on to my father's house here, where I can escape when I need to, where I can continue to see my mother's high school landscape over the bed and study the tall, skinny pines that surround the house? Maybe the fish will take to the rest of us the way they took to my father and he, in the broad universe beyond, will know as only the spirit world might know, the way we love him and carry on. The way we carry on here in his little house on his remote northern lake. This key in my hand. Every May, I can take it out of the top drawer, head down to the lake and start up the motor. Take the boat out, as my father did every early spring, just to follow the shore, cross the middle, review the new season happening yet again.

But, of course, something will go wrong. The motor will sputter and, unlike my father, I will not know what to do, how to jiggle the right lever or gizmo. The boat will need maintenance. And this house too. The old plumbing, old wiring, old roof. My god. In the city I keep an entire notebook of resources to help with everything from the ongoing electrical to the occasional raccoon up from the creek, whole pages of neatly taped business cards. Because living breaks down at every turn. Tell me if I'm wrong. I put the key on its labeled paper back into the drawer.

Behind it, I find an envelope, plain white, smudged, old. I reach in and take out a rough scrap of thick paper, almost cardboard, torn without care, as if in a rush. On it I see just one line, written in a large, loopy scrawl, that says:

Do not find me.

Find who? The writer signed no name, put no return address on the envelope, left no indication. Yet my father saved it for me to find.

On this matter I truly know nothing. I let my father go without my knowing anything about a person he wanted to find. Worse, a person who did not want my father to find him or her. What a blow this note must have been, this stern order to be left alone. I reach for my phone, like a reflex, what I do when I need information. I poke at the icons and get answers, directions. Anything.

"Aunt Bella? Can you hear me? The connection is not so clear."

"Margaret, dear, is that you? Goodness is something wrong? You sound so distressed. Is something wrong up there?"

"Auntie, I have to ask you about my father in New York, you know, years ago. When you were both young and you made your recordings, you know, back then."

"Oh, that was a time, Margaret, you cannot imagine. So different. So gay and lovely then. How we all had our dreams. And the little clubs, our parties, we tried so hard then, we really did. We reached, dear, if you can imagine. How we reached to be something."

"But my father, Auntie, was my father in love? Did someone break his heart? He never said. He wouldn't say about New York. So I don't know." Suddenly, I am crying. I cannot stop myself. I am crying so hard I have to quit talking.

"Margaret, dear, why are you asking? If he didn't want to say, I don't think it's my place. Oh, Gigi," she trails off, and then she also cries.

"I found a note in his handkerchief drawer. It says, *Do not find me.*"

"Oh no," Auntie Bella wails back. "Oh Margaret, dear, I did not think—"

I have to wait a full minute as she sobs from her condominium there in the strange land of Manzanillo, Mexico, where I am certain she is looking out this very minute at the bluest water imaginable, just as I stand here looking out the kitchen window at the wide white of Lost Lake in November.

Then she says, "Poor Gigi. My poor dear Gigi."

"Auntie?" The line is dead. In the utterly silent house, I sit on my mother's tweedy chair, her last decorating gesture, still holding the note that I cannot translate and the phone that is supposed to connect me to anyone or anything I choose. But it cannot connect me to my father's past. Not even Auntie Isabella will connect me to my father's past.

I'm so tired. I just want to close my eyes and know the answers. Or if I cannot know, I want to be left alone. I want to rest. I turn off my phone. I do not turn on the light. Instead I drift away, letting the many tall, skinny pines surrounding the house guard me as they do. And as night comes, I sleep.

TWO

1961

They brought in their broken baubles, their cheap stones, and hand-me-down pearl chokers and he fixed them. Gigi, the man who could be in show business if he'd only try, his pale blue eyes and surprising good grace. The girls loved him, especially when the audition went badly and their hairdos flattened under their rain scarves, or they suddenly realized, just then on some ordinary Tuesday in New York City, that they weren't going to make it after all. They were not the next Ava Gardner or Lauren Bacall or Marilyn. They were just a Susan or Nancy from nowhere, who couldn't get a good part to save her soul. And Gigi would look into them deeply and smile in his good-natured way, handle a busted bracelet like something worthy of his time.

"You have to come to my Valentine's party," Billy Jo said, tipping her head at an alluring angle, the way he saw the showgirls do, though it didn't change anything. They still were whoever they had always been, the good daughter who never stayed out past curfew, the babysitter who saved all her change to buy a train ticket out, the fusspot who wouldn't wear a stocking that didn't have a straight seam. They were who they were, just as he was what he'd always been. His mother used to tell him that he was all eyes. A watcher. He observed. That's what he did.

Certainly he'd observed Billy Jo's eagerness and need. "You'll love my friends, I just know you will, and they'll bring you all their business too. You can't believe how those girls break things. And

I know some nice guys too." She'd giggled. "But I don't know if they break things."

He said he would come to her party. But no party, however sublime, could compete with the exhilaration he felt walking home in the hustle of a city that never ceased to entertain and stimulate him. When the February sun dropped behind buildings in mid-afternoon, he didn't need to glance at a clock to know where he stood in time. He'd come to New York from a small town near the Canadian border where the skyline was never tall enough to hide much of anything, let alone the giant sweep of the sun. When the afternoon shifted suddenly to early evening, he would put all his work in small boxes, roll up his tools, and lock the drawers of his table.

He'd lived in New York for more than two years, in a third-floor walk up on Thirty-Second off Lexington. It took him almost an hour to get home from the time he left the jewelry store at Eighty-First and Madison Avenue, an amazing wonderful hour every day. These older women with their little dogs and the dogs with their hairdos just like the showgirls. Ribbons. Women wearing furs and hats with feathers. Men in such fine wools, not ever wrinkled and their hats, too, with more feathers, tucked into a brim, probably coming from an extinct tropical bird somewhere. Babies wrapped in matching knits—bonnets and booties, their blankets new, not worn or remade. Store-bought new. That's how the walk home began. And dark-skinned maids in white caps looking like nurses, but their shoes telling the story of Upper East Side maids. And everyone with purpose. Gigi loved this total absorption people had in wherever it was they were going, whatever it was they were doing. No idle strolling, no searching for another's eye. Not up here. Up here folks were busy.

By Forty-Ninth Street they were more than busy. They were crazed. Hailing cabs, catching buses, hurrying into a door, out of a door, shop girls laughing wildly at something just said, midlevel employees fighting the weather in not quite the right clothes. No scarf in the cold. A scarf out of control in the wind. Always a bum or two mumbling about money, a nut or two yelling about Jesus or the Russians. All the buildings bright with lights of every kind. He couldn't believe his luck. That he was here. That after more than twenty years in a flat, remote place, he had landed in a city that overflowed with color and spark. He still couldn't believe his luck.

"It's Gigi," Billy Jo squealed when she opened the door to her apartment that turned out to be every bit as tiny and old as his own. But dozens of people had crowded into her two rooms, holding their drinks and smoking their cigarettes. "This is Gigi Paulo, everyone. Some of you know his sister, Bella Paul. She was in the Broadway show *Christine* last year."

"Didn't that close after a week?" someone in the room threw out.

"Gigi repairs all my jewels," Billy Jo continued. "At this marvelous shop on Eighty-First and Madison." She smiled at him and all of them, as though she alone had made these good things occur, high-end shops and jewelry repairs, and handsome men in her doorway. Gigi slid out of his coat to take hold of a glass of spiked red punch.

"Some kind of name," the man next to him said.

"Short for Giovanni."

"Why don't you just call yourself John?" The man inhaled his Camel.

"My older sisters tagged me back when. I don't mind."

But the man, who had not bothered to introduce himself, didn't let go. "Doesn't it bother you that there's that movie out there, *Gigi*, and that song? That French schoolgirl?"

"I don't mind," Gigi said again and eased away to another corner of the room, where a card table held plates of sandwiches and cupcakes.

"I did it all myself," Billy Jo called to him as she squeezed by with a tray of cheese-filled triangles. She'd decorated her apartment with red streamers that did not hide the cracked walls, the bruised woodwork, and chipped radiators. Still Billy Jo had scored a nonworking fireplace, where she had stacked logs that would never burn. Over her mantle she'd hung an enormous mirror, almost as big as the fireplace itself, an old mirror maybe salvaged from someone else's trash. The surface had been damaged in one corner. Staring at the dark, chipped spot, Gigi considered how he could fix it, remake the corner, match the old paint.

"So you're Bella Paul's brother?" Two girls stood in front of him, holding their red punch drinks, one in satin, the other in sequins.

"Yes, she's my sister."

"Oh my gosh," the one in sequins said, "I went through that whole *Finian's Rainbow* tryout with her last year and she was so good." She turned to her friend. "His sister sings like, I can't say, you can't imagine. I was sure she'd get in."

"She has a beautiful voice," Gigi agreed. "All my sisters can sing."

"Not you?" the other girl asked, her chin down and her eyelashes up.

He shook his head, as the girl in the sequins went on, "So they gave us a page from 'How Are Things in Glocca Morra?' and his sister, she sings this song so perfectly, I'm crying, I really am, 'is that little brook still leaping there,' she's singing and I'm thinking stop crying you ape or you'll clog your own voice, which of course I did and then your sister didn't even get in. I couldn't believe it.

What's she doing now anyway? I haven't seen her. Mother Mary she can sing."

"She's working the hat counter at Bonwit Teller," he answered. The other girl kept looking up at him from under her eyelashes.

"But she's not in a show?"

"She's trying out. She sings at home, takes classes."

"Don't we all," said the girl under the eyelashes.

"I wish I'd tried out for *The Fantasticks*. Who'd have thought. No scenery, a narrator, off-Broadway. But this girl I know told me the music is great, who cares if it's off-Broadway. She tries out. She gets the understudy lead, for god's sake. And now it's all anyone's talking about."

"Which sandwich do you like best?" Billy Jo yelled to him above the din. "Did you try the egg salad? I'm so darn good at egg salad." She slid two egg salad triangles onto his plate and as she did, he saw her distracted by a girl in the far corner of the room, just inside the door. For a minute, all Gigi could see was the top of the girl's head, a frenzied heap of brown hair, a messy look not at all in style. He stayed where he was under the red streamers, eating egg salad triangles and watching Billy Jo work her way to the door, where she stood talking to the dark-haired girl. He set his plate on the mantle and followed Billy Jo's path through the crowd. As he neared the door, Billy Jo turned and Gigi saw the new girl's face, and at that very second, he felt his knees loosen so suddenly, he had to grab Billy Jo's arm for stability.

"Gigi, this is my new friend, Corrine. She's French. Her mother's French anyway. Does that make you French, Corrine?"

"I know you," Gigi said, hardly moving.

The girl lifted an eyebrow. "I don't think so," she answered. "I remember faces."

"Gigi has a great face," Billy Jo gushed. "We tell him he should be in show business. Try out for something, but he just gives us that halfway grin. See? Like he's doing now." She jammed his arm with her own. "You're our phantom, Gigi. Our Italian phantom out of nowhere."

"Are you out of nowhere?" the girl asked. Her face showed almost no emotion, her eyes wide and as dark as her hair.

"I grew up in Northern Minnesota, land of ten thousand lakes. Open pit mines and lakes."

"And cold," Billy Jo said. "Maybe forty below in the winter his sister told me."

"You are not a lone phantom then?" the girl Corrine asked. "There are others?"

"His sister is Bella Paul. She sings like Julie Andrews."

"So she is a star?"

"No," Gigi answered, "she sells hats."

"I can't stand it," Billy Jo said. "Her time will come, Gigi. Your sister's going to make it. Oh my gosh, I've got to put out more punch." She pushed into the crowd of her friends and left Gigi to Corrine.

He had recovered slightly, but still felt unsteady. "You are in show business too?" he asked. His back was to the room, so all he saw was this girl named Corrine, so familiar to him, small and strong looking, her serious face and layers of fringed scarves around her shoulders and neck, like the peasant in a Christmas tale, like a Dickens orphan.

"I act," she said.

"Are you in a play?"

She didn't answer, but looked around the room for something or someone, maybe only for an answer to his question. Finally, not finding what she needed, she came back to him. "I didn't know Italians had blue eyes."

"Some Viking warrior, I suppose, trying to conquer the hill towns." He wanted her to smile.

"Like one of those ten thousand lakes where you come from. I would say." Then, abruptly, she added, "I am pleased to have met you," and moved away toward the card table of sandwiches, where for a long while Gigi watched her eat and down whole glasses of Billy Jo's strong punch. She didn't seem to know anyone else or care. She was another in Billy Jo's collection, coming from somewhere, trying to be something more.

Of course the girl did not know him. But Gigi had seen her before, unmistakably her, sitting in a bar near Penn Station the day after he arrived in New York. Coming off the train, he'd stored one of his suitcases in a locker so he could walk to his sister's apartment, where he planned to stay until he found a place of his own. He'd stopped for a small lunch and to watch the people, all these surprising people everywhere. At home in Minnesota he'd stayed away from bars, places where men talked too loud and drank too much, all of a cut, raised on the tundra to live a man's life of mining and hunting, sporting and drinking. None of them interested Gigi. But every block in New York seemed to have a door into another world with characters of all sorts. Gigi didn't even need to talk to feel connected, fascinated, carried along in that bar near Penn Station at a table in the corner. He drank a glass of cheap wine and ate a sandwich of some kind, took in the other patrons, their postures and manners, the scuffed shoes and array of hats.

He didn't see the girl come into the bar that first day in New York. He looked up from his plate and she was there at the table closest to the door with scarves wrapped around her in layers of color and fringe. She wore gloves and when she finally removed them, she revealed delicate, white hands that waved the bartender her way, gestured her order, then waved him away again.

For almost an hour Gigi nursed a second glass of wine and then two cups of coffee just to watch her. She ate a bowl of soup with a plate of bread. She drank two beers. Then she asked for more bread and spread it with chunks of butter. Through all this she never looked in Gigi's direction, but alternated between quick glances at the door and a meditative concentration on her food and drink. Then she left as swiftly as she'd come, without any fuss to her departure. He thought he'd kept his eyes on her constantly, yet she slipped out between breaths, between blinks. And he could not follow because he had to pay, get his coat and hat off the hook, and he knew he'd be too late. She was lost to him the instant she walked out the door.

He returned to that bar near Penn Station every day for two weeks. He was looking for work then, and between visits to jewelry and department stores, he'd go in for lunch or coffee or anything that might mean he would see her again. The day he was offered a job at the shop on Eighty-First and Madison Avenue, he took a bus to Midtown one more time. After sitting through the noon rush and even the lull that followed the noon rush, he approached the bartender, the same middle-aged man who had served the girl on Gigi's first visit. "You make a good cup of coffee," he started, but the man only glanced at him. "Is this your bar?" The bartender stopped working to squint at Gigi. "It's a good spot," Gigi added, and though he could tell he'd already alienated the man, he kept going, his tone even, but his confidence wavering. "I saw a very pretty girl here awhile back. With curly hair and lots of scarves around her. You seemed to know her, so I wanted to ask." He didn't want to smile for fear of appearing frivolous or disrespectful. When the bartender finally looked up, he met Gigi's eyes directly and said, "Maybe you better just pay up." He moved down the bar to another patron.

It should have been over then. But some part of Gigi had attached to the image of that girl. At first he searched for her in the people walking the streets of New York. He'd hope that she was entering the jewelry shop every time the door opened. He found an apartment just blocks from the bar, thinking he might see her in the neighborhood. Then that gave way to occasional, passionate dreams, dreams in which she came to him silently, always wearing those scarves, the rest of her body as white and expressive as the hands he'd watched in the bar. He could not conjure her. She found his dreams on far and random nights, so that he'd awaken always with the joy of her still with him, real though elusive. As real and elusive as the moon, he thought.

Gigi supposed he'd always been a bit fanciful. It ran in the family— his father's light humor, his mother's fondness for whimsy, his sisters singing, making up plays in the backyard, devising new identities for themselves at every phase of life. He'd created elaborate schemes as a child. By the time he turned thirteen, he'd been a fighter pilot, a police detective, a soldier captured by any number of vile enemies, a mole living beneath his mother's garden, a prizefighter, and a tiger trainer in the circus. He'd let himself be carried away by radio dramas, books, gossip around town, the narratives of all those songs his sisters played on the phonograph. A naked girl with colored scarves at her neck did not seem so far removed from the other worlds he'd explored. But this time, the fantasy had stayed so long as to become a part of him. He'd known her intimately for so long, he could almost not pretend she was a stranger at Billy Jo's party, a hungry girl who said she was an actress. He could almost not pretend.

⁓

Once again she left before he could follow. She'd been able to flow through Billy Jo's friends like a trickle of water between river rocks. He saw her there by the sandwiches. He stepped away from the door for more punch, and she was gone.

"So," Billy Jo beamed at him, "don't I have great friends?"

"How do you know the girl with the scarves?"

Billy Jo still grinned. She had a way of continuing to smile as though frozen in the happy moment, her red lipstick perfectly outlining her white teeth, all still smiling. "Corrine?" Billy Jo relaxed her face. "Actually, I met her at the theater supply store on Thirty-Seventh. I don't know what I was doing there. Feather boa or something, and Corrine was asking the clerk about wigs or hair dye or something. So we talked."

"She says she's an actress," Gigi said.

"Me too," Billy Jo answered, moving back into her oversized smile. Then someone at the door called to her, and she turned her red grin that way, hurrying to say good-bye to her guests. Gigi picked up paper plates and napkins, stacked punch glasses in Billy Jo's sink, and waited for the last person to leave. Billy Jo dropped onto her sagging sofa and kicked off her high heels. "Thanks, Gigi."

"Did you have fun?" he asked, though he already knew the answer.

"God, I love a party." She scanned the messy room. "Eating and drinking and just playing around all night. Don't you love my streamers too?"

Gigi sat down next to her. "You're a good egg, Billy. My mom would have liked you."

"So she's gone?" She looked at him intently, ready to be sympathetic.

"She died six years ago. Then my dad died too. That's why I came out here. I was alone and Isabella was here. She said it was the place for me."

"New York is the place, isn't it? Who can be alone in New York City? Hey, you want to go listen to some music?"

"Now?"

"Live it up, Gigi." Billy Jo put on her boots and bundled against the cold. Outside, she said, "This has been the worst winter, hasn't it? But there are places in the Village that stay open all night no matter what." Then, as they walked, she told him tales of her auditions since she arrived in New York in 1959. That's when Gigi had arrived too, and it struck him, listening to Billy's many escapades, that he'd lived so quietly in comparison. He wasn't a show business type like Billy. He didn't aspire to fame, only to a certain joy, to the day's sweetness, its undercurrent of meaning. In a way, he'd come to New York with no more ambition than to live the rounded, whole life he believed his parents had lived. To work well, eat well, take in the weather and seasons, the angles of light. But to do it where the streets bustled and the buildings rose like gods.

He liked his routines. After work he walked home through the city's bustle, picked up food to cook, drank his one glass of red wine, and watched the evening news. Sometimes he went out to a movie or walked over to the Morgan Library to read. For a short while he dated a librarian named Molly, who had red hair and so many freckles her nose looked brown. But though he made an effort to charm her, his heart was never in it. He felt relieved when she moved to Boston.

Girls always interested him. He'd grown up with four sisters, so he felt comfortable with girls. He thought he understood them better than other men did. But he'd never been in love. He didn't think he had.

"You go to this place a lot?" Gigi asked, as they crossed MacDougal to the Gaslight.

"Someone's always here," she answered. "Maybe not your sister, but other girls I know. It's a place, you know. It's something."

The smoky café pulsed, people drinking, talking, crowding around their tables. A skinny boy stood on stage singing through his nose, wailing without shame. "He's terrible," Billy Jo said into Gigi's ear and stuck her tongue out. Gigi nodded, but his eye was on the audience, looking for a girl with unruly curls, wrapped in fringed shawls. He saw Corrine sitting in a far corner, fixed on the boy singing. Gigi nudged Billy Jo and pointed.

"She left my party to listen to him?" Billy Jo hollered into his ear, clearly insulted that she'd come second to this unsatisfying performer.

Gigi found chairs along the wall and carried one after another to Corrine's spot at the edge of the room, where he and Billy Jo sat down on either side of her, though she only glanced at them. In the dim light and thick smoke, Gigi could study the girl as he had never been able to do before, every feature so finely honed, the lashes so perfectly curled upward, the pale skin set off by the wild dark hair. He'd never seen a girl who looked like this. Every woman and girl he knew at home and in New York tamed her hair into some kind of shape, a coif or bob or bun or braid. Or this new hairdo the president's wife wore, puffed and smooth. Billy Jo called it teasing and demonstrated once by pushing the comb backward to the roots of her hair. "You're killing it," he'd said, shocked. "It's the thing," she'd answered. "Mrs. Kennedy does it." But Corrine tried for no order at all. Her hair grew in large random curls, and that's how she left it.

Seeing her up close he was quite sure she wore no makeup like Billy Jo, whose red mouth glistened even in the darkened room. Corrine dressed in wild scraps of clothing. Tonight she wore a loose, heavy skirt, a sweater on top of another sweater, a man's storm coat like the one his father wore every cold day of Gigi's childhood, tweedy and large. The coat lay over the back of her chair. But the fringed scarves around her neck remained, one lemon yellow, the other blue plaid.

"Who is this guy?" Billy Jo yelled out to Corrine, but was ignored. Billy caught Gigi's eye and shrugged, making him laugh, which prompted Corrine to look his way, to meet his stare and hold it. She seemed able to contain her every emotion without a flicker of revelation. Then just as suddenly, she looked back at the singer. A minute later the crowd clapped, the boy bowed, and Corrine slid her arms into her coat.

"Don't go," Billy Jo said, "we're just getting started." But Corrine went. She hugged Billy Jo with one arm, nodded to Gigi, and headed toward the door.

"We've got to see her home," Gigi said, panicked that she was slipping away from him again. "Good lord, it's the middle of the night." He hurried after her, but on MacDougal, he saw no trace of Corrine. Her obvious knowledge of the city, the streets, her uncanny ability to disappear overwhelmed him.

When he stomped back into the café, he asked Billy Jo, "Where the devil does this girl go to all the time?"

"All the time? You only just met her. Anyway, that's Corrine."

"She shouldn't even be out there all alone." He shook his head, disgusted with something, himself or the girl, he couldn't be sure.

"Have a coffee," Billy Jo said, shoving a cup across the table. "I ordered one for you."

He didn't want the coffee. He didn't like the Gaslight. All these people looking like bums and that skinny boy getting ready to sing another lousy song. He wanted the New York of his longing, the pretty busy dreamers he saw every day on the streets or the rich, bossy customers at the shop or the excited immigrants running their corner groceries and laundries. Not this night world, modern music he supposed, somebody's new idea of music. "Does anyone ever sing the blues at this place?" he yelled to Billy Jo over the noise.

She flashed him her red smile. "I'm sure. You just have to be here at the right time."

He tried after that to be there at the right time. With equal parts determination and misery, Gigi went to the Gaslight many nights over the next two weeks. He gave up evenings in his apartment reading magazines and newspapers. He gave up television dramas and his well-constructed private space for the possibility of reconnecting with the girl Corrine. He didn't even know her last name. At the Gaslight he sat through countless sets of folk songs about pet dragons, sad men on trains, and rowing boats. He didn't see Corrine or even Billy Jo. And he never heard the blues.

In his apartment he'd started a collection of vocalists who sang the songs he now associated with his New York, a city of enterprise and transformation, of love and loss. On a shelf he made himself out of discarded lumber, he stored his record albums of Sarah Vaughan, Rosemary Clooney, Peggy Lee, Ella, and Billie. He dusted them before putting them on his turntable and dusted the needle too for a most clear and heartbreaking sound. After suffering at the café for so many unproductive nights, Gigi finally decided to return to his music at home. On his way back from work, he stopped to buy meat at the Polish grocery down the block and made a pot of sauce the way his mother had taught him, with almost an entire bottle of red wine and just the right measure of tomato.

He'd lived in this third story walk-up since his second month in New York, thanking his lucky stars daily for the airy space he'd found. Long and almost narrow, the apartment had three tall windows facing south with a ten-foot-long radiator underneath. He'd placed a sofa and bed in front of the radiator with a shared table and lamp between them. On the opposite wall a makeshift kitchen had been added at some point in time with a sink, stove, and refrigerator all in a tidy row. At a junk store he'd found an enormous round table, made of oak, but badly battered. For weeks he'd sanded the table until it was smooth again, tightened the wobbly bolts in its legs and then painted it red like a fire engine. That table stood near his makeshift kitchen. He kept one African violet in a pot in the middle of the table, deep purple against the brilliant red. His mother loved African violets. It kept her in the room for him, and over the two years the plant had grown large in the indirect light of his dirty, barred windows.

But for how much he loved this one room, it was the bathroom off the makeshift kitchen that he thought to be his jewel in the crown, for it was a third as big as the rest of the apartment, huge by city standards, with a built-in cupboard on one whole wall, big enough to store his towels and sheets, his clothes and even his tools. The doors opened seven feet high, so that he felt to be a child again in a world much more grand than he had a right to enter. His sister loved this bathroom, which also had a large claw-foot tub, where she came sometimes just to soak in bubbles and pamper herself.

Gigi had never lived alone before, and he found it suited him, this one room and bath with its high ceilings and tall windows. He liked surveying his territory in one glance, seeing his bed as he ate his dinner, watching the outside lights reflect in his mirror as he fell asleep. And he found apartment life reassuring, the clatter of feet going up and down stairs, a door slamming now and then, some unidentified person laughing hysterically in the hallway, even cooking smells, the whole texture of day-to-day living comforted him, made him feel part of the larger world.

He was almost ready to eat when the phone rang, startling him out of a reverie about the cheese he was grating—his mother's jar of grated cheese always ready to go, the twelve-pound rounds she bought to split with his aunties, the crumbs she left behind for him to nibble. "Gigi, it's me." He heard the agitation in Billy Jo's voice. "Corrine just called asking where you lived. She didn't say why, but I thought you wouldn't mind, so I gave her your address and she's on her way. Did I do the wrong thing?"

"She's coming here?"

"I gave her your address. I didn't know if I should."

"It's fine, Billy. It's fine."

"I need to come by the shop. My watch is skipping minutes, Gigi. Whole minutes of my life."

Gigi's hands shook as he hung up. His dinner now looked impossible, he had no appetite, but covered the bowl and set it on the warm stove. Then he opened his bottle of wine, put Frank Sinatra on the phonograph, and sat at his red table to wait for the girl Corrine.

He'd played both sides of the album and was sliding it into its jacket when he heard the knock. She appeared as she always did, calm and disheveled, mildly disinterested yet alert. "Billy Jo called you." She stated this fact. "Did you cook?" she asked, her nose tilted upward to smell the spaghetti and sauce sitting covered on the stove.

"Would you like to eat? Or have a glass of wine? Would you like a glass of wine?"

"I didn't know a man would live this way," she said. Her eyes moved around the room. "All this color. With a plant on the table."

"I'm Italian," he replied, thinking it might be funny. But she didn't laugh.

"I could eat with you," she said. "I could have a glass of wine."

Gigi pulled out a chair for her and for once she took up his signal and sat down at the table. Then he set out plates and the mismatched silver he'd bought at the secondhand store and two of his mother's cloth napkins. He poured wine for them and heaped spaghetti onto the two plates. He didn't talk to her, but he saw that she was looking at everything in his apartment, her eyes wandering slowly around again and again. When he sat down to eat with her, she said a small thank you to him and nothing more. She cut the noodles and put one forkful after another into her mouth, chewing quietly. Gigi watched her in fascination, the way he had when he first spotted her in the bar. She ate so much and with great method. She ate with amazing purpose, he thought. His mother would have loved the way she ate.

Finished with her food, she sat back in the chair. "Thank you," she said.

"Would you like more?" Gigi asked, thinking he'd like to continue watching her eat. Instead she picked up her plate and brought it to the sink, where she rinsed it completely before turning back to him.

"I'd like to stay actually."

"Here?"

"With you," she said so casually that Gigi was not sure exactly what she meant. "I'd like to stay with you."

Gigi was unprepared for this. "You want me to," she added. Still she didn't smile. She waited for his answer as though they were negotiating a contract, then asked, "Shall I stay?" Her question held in the room between them, until Gigi walked over to his makeshift kitchen and turned off the lights over the sink and round table. Then he moved across his room to turn off the lamp between his bed and his sofa, until the only light left came from the city outside, the bounce of urban lighting across his floor and the flicker of that same light over his bed.

Neither of them talked. The girl came toward him, unraveling her scarves and removing her clothes. Underneath she wore loose silk panties, old-fashioned, with buttons up the side and nothing else. She stepped past him to the bed, where she folded the bedspread open and slipped between the sheets without invitation. All of this startled him. As did her arms, more thin than the Corrine of his dreams, and more flawed he saw, as he sat down on the bed beside her. She had small red bumps, some kind of rash that he did not think was new, but perhaps chronic, bumps she'd had when she was five and twelve and through the years to now.

He touched the blotched skin on her arms. Slowly, ceremoniously, he took off his outer clothing and lay down next to her. She didn't smell like flowers or fruit as he had fancied she would, but sweaty, needing a bath he thought, as he touched her, still with hesitation. He did not know her. He had thought about her for two years, but never like this. Never with her silk shorts and bony arms, never with a rash or this distracting lack of joy. Abruptly she pulled him down and rolled on top. She licked and bit him, and Gigi let her, though he didn't feel happy as he did in his dreams. His eyes focused on the city light that darted around them. He heard the gurgle of water in the old radiator, comforted by that, even in the presence of the girl he'd wanted for so long. He kept searching for her face in the dark, but she turned one way and another, a girl on her own with an idea and a technique, maybe some desire, if only he could see it. Their encounter lasted long enough for the building he lived in to settle into that late-night stillness he'd come to know. But Corrine never met his eyes nor stopped moving over and around him. She made no sounds, but remained lost in a world she was creating, her own movie scene or a cut of live, audacious theater with the heroine so beautifully busy at love she had no time to notice the effect she was having, how the audience might be gasping or gripping the arms of the theater seats in vicarious pleasure. Then she kissed him softly on the mouth and rolled away from him.

In the morning when he awoke, she was already gone. He wandered the room looking for some sign, a note or forgotten sock, a glove, but Corrine had left nothing behind her. She had managed to dress in the dark room and open his double lock to go back out onto the streets, where she would have found her way home the way he knew she did, instinctively taking the right avenue to the right alley to wherever it was she lived.

"Billy Jo," he said to his friend on the other end of the telephone line, "do you know where Corrine lives?"

"Gigi, is it you? It's the middle of the night. I can't believe I'm awake."

"It's seven in the morning. I'm sorry to wake you up, but I have to head out soon and I wondered if you know where Corrine lives."

He could hear Billy Jo sigh. "Did she come over last night?"

"She did," he said, hoping he would not have to explain more.

"I don't know. Corrine, she's spooky. I don't know where she lives. She doesn't have a number, always calls me, never invites me over or says boo about her life except that her mother is French."

"What's her name? You must know that."

"She has a stage name, like your sister. I forget what she said. I forget what it is."

"So where does she act? This acting she does, where is it?"

Billy Jo didn't answer. He could hear her rattling in her kitchen. "Gigi? Are you in love with Corrine or something? Because, honestly, I know other girls you might like more. Even at my Valentine's party. One of my friends liked you a lot that night. And she knows Bella too. Jeannie's her name. Really, she's so much fun. You know, lively and fun." She stopped and banged around on the other end some more. "I can't think until I have coffee," she said. "You're so sweet, Gigi. You could choose, you know what I mean? All the girls love you." She dropped the phone and muttered something he could not hear before she picked it up again and said, "Corrine's dark. She's my friend too and I love her for being so peculiar, but she's dark, Gigi. She won't make you laugh."

"I'll think about what you're saying," he responded, not wanting her to worry or get involved. "But do you know where she works or acts or takes lessons?"

"That's my point, Gigi," Billy Jo said. "I don't know anything. Actually I do. I know she'll show up. Now she's got your address, she'll come back. Or you'll see her in the neighborhood. Or she'll call me. Maybe she'll show up at the jewelry store. Oh my gosh, I have to come by today with that watch. See you later." He heard another crash and Billy Jo hung up.

Before he left for work, Gigi washed the dinner dishes, but he did not make the bed. He could not bring himself to disturb the natural disarray of his night with Corrine. It hadn't been what he'd hoped or what he wanted, but she'd been here and all over him and he had to admit that meant something. She'd liked his spaghetti and his violet on the red table. She slept in silk shorts with tiny buttons his agile fingers struggled to undo. Her hair felt softer than he had thought it would, and her skin felt rougher. She had cold feet, sharp elbows, and purpose. It must mean something.

Corrine didn't return that week or the next. Not seeing her ruined Gigi's life during that time. She was all he could think about and he looked for her constantly. Even his treasured walk home changed. Instead of noticing the well-dressed babies and women's hats, the smooth faces of the smooth men, his eyes scanned every passerby, every small crowd waiting for the light to change, every window and doorway looking for Corrine. He became an obsessed birder waiting on just one rare bird. He stayed home at night in case she came to his door again. He kept his lights low, a wine bottle open, the bed mussed and ready.

"You're so cranky," Billy Jo commented when she stopped by the store to pick up her watch. "It isn't like you." She stood staring at him as he continued to work. "It's Corrine, isn't it? She's making you cranky. I told you she's not the girl for you, Gigi. Let me fix you up with Jeannie. She'll make you laugh."

He had no interest in Jeannie, whoever she was, or anyone other than Corrine. He wanted another chance with her. Now that he'd had time to consider her driven approach to love, he wanted to see if he could match her or calm her or be more connected to her through the long hours of a night. That's what he wanted, another chance. He could scarcely think of anything else. At work he was back to glancing up every time the door opened, as he'd done when he first found Corrine and lost her, two years ago or more. He was right back where he started, searching out a phantom, only now he knew the feel of her. He knew her flaws and oddities, which only made him want her more.

A late March thunderstorm raged all Saturday. Gigi didn't have to work, so he stayed home and cleaned his apartment. The knock at the door came softly. When he opened it there she was, completely wet, one fringed scarf wrapped and dripping on her head, her face red from the wind, her right eye blackened and cut.

"What happened to you?" Gigi cried and ushered her inside, where she sat at the table, reached for the purple violet, and clutched it with both hands. She answered none of Gigi's queries as to what had happened to her. She didn't look at him or talk, but over the next hour, she did what he said. She took off her wet clothes, sat in a hot bath, and afterward put on a robe and socks. They ate. They drank wine.

The following morning Corrine sat up in bed and smiled at him. "I slept so well," she said. She pulled her fingers through her hair as a way of combing, then fluffed the whole mass back up again.

"Maybe you'd like to stay for a while," Gigi offered.

"How do you keep that violet blooming?" she asked, touching the plant's petals along the edges. Then suddenly she said, "I'll be back. Don't go anywhere," and bolted out the door, leaving her coat and fringed scarves behind. He heard her on the steps, heard the door slam below.

An hour later Corrine returned with a few belongings in a soft leather bag, polished, almost new. He didn't wonder then how she would come to carry her clothing in such a handsome vehicle, but he noticed its quality. She settled in with the resolve he'd come to expect, and he watched the way he always did, surprised that a person like her existed, not sure what she'd do next, yet with a sense of knowing her anyway, of being pulled in her direction no matter what.

She said little. When he lived with his sisters, those years growing up in a house too small for seven people, they'd talked all the time, muttered and yelled out across the whole house to each other or to him. And when they weren't talking, they sang. He loved the meaningless chatter of people living together. Nobody really listened all that much. But the parade went along, holding to a rhythm, keeping to the sunny side, noisy and good-natured.

Corrine said little, but she stayed. When Gigi came home from work, Corrine merely glanced up from whatever she was doing. She seemed content to do nothing all day, to watch his television or flip through the magazines he bought for her, busy women's magazines with stories in them and the season's fashions. She didn't want to leave the apartment. When he came home, he put on music while he cooked, and she stood near him reading the album jackets. "You really like these sad singers, don't you?" she asked the second night she was there. "They're mostly colored."

He explained how he'd discovered them when he moved to New York, how they epitomized the city's rhythm to him. "These singers, they pull me in," he said. "All their longing, their deep voices." He sang along to the Sarah Vaughan song playing on his phonograph. "Make yourself comfortable, baby," he crooned, but Corrine wrinkled her nose.

"Not for me," she said, picking at a tear in the album cover.

"You prefer that skinny kid at the Gaslight," Gigi countered, noticing how much his remark sounded like an accusation.

"I do," she answered.

"How can you like music about trains and highways, lemon trees—." He searched for images from the dreadful songs he'd heard at the coffee house all those nights when he was hoping to see Corrine again. "And jails," he added, before he saw her unhappy stare from across the room.

"It's better than women wailing about love." She went into the bathroom and closed the door.

Other moments were easier. Sometimes she asked him about the food, why he added the wine when he did or dipped the fish in flour and egg before he fried them. She liked to turn the violet on his table this way and that, catching it at different angles. One day she told him she was writing a script for a character she wanted to play, the queen of some far-off country, but she didn't ask him to read it. He saw only her large scrawling letters and loopy lines on the page, and after that day, he never saw it again.

For more than a week she did not reach for him in bed, but settled herself against the wall. "I'm still healing," she said. He'd taken to holding her hand and massaging it, circling over every bone and joint. One night he put her baby finger in his mouth, but she quickly pulled it back and kept to her own space by the wall.

As April burst into color all over the city, Gigi focused his life on Corrine. Billy Jo called once, but he evaded her questions, said he was battling a sore throat, promised he'd call again soon. Then his sister arrived for one of her hour-long baths on an afternoon when Gigi was working. She let herself in with her own key, and there stood Corrine, just feet from the door, with her wild hair, baggy clothes, and black eye. Isabella dropped her bag and fell against the wall. "I had no idea," she said. "Nobody's ever here when I come."

"Who are you?" Corrine asked.

Isabella recovered her best manners, lifted herself high, and extended her hand. "I'm Gigi's sister, Isabella. I go by Bella Paul professionally."

"The singer," Corrine said. "You look like him."

"Yes." Isabella waited for Corrine to identify herself. She hadn't talked to Gigi in a couple of weeks she realized. Something clearly had gone on for him during that time that this waiflike girl should be wandering around his apartment while he was at work.

"I'm Corrine."

"I had no idea," Isabella repeated. "Are you hurt? Your eye—it's painful?"

"Gigi looks after me," Corrine said. "Like his violet there," she added, cocking her head toward the red table.

"Goodness. And he's at work?"

Corrine nodded.

"Do you work?"

"I am an actress."

"I see."

"I'm learning the Method," Corrine said with some pride. "To go deep and really feel."

"Well, of course. Of course. Goodness. Actually I'm here for a bath. I love Gigi's tub—if I'm not troubling you."

Isabella had Gigi's same blue eyes, clear and sympathetic. Her long brown hair framed a round, yet regal face, a face with broad cheekbones, a wide forehead and the sculpted chin of an ancient queen. Corrine stared at her without blinking.

"So," Isabella said then, "I'll be in the bathroom an hour or so, if you want to use it before I go in."

When Gigi came home at six, he found his sister sitting on the sofa with her hair wrapped in a towel, concentrating intensely on Corrine, who was walking in slow, heavy strides across the room. When she reached her destination, her posture remained weary, as though she had spent hours in arduous travel, her shoulders curved forward, her head low and her knees bent. In this manner she turned to Isabella and bowed.

"Bravo," Isabella called, clapping her hands and sitting taller. "Corrine has been demonstrating her art, Gigi."

Corrine emerged from her bit of theater and acknowledged him. "I walked the desert," she said. "I wanted to show your sister how I find inner motivation."

"So," Isabella continued, "she has crossed the desert in deep feeling. She has lost herself to the journey, and I felt it. I did. Her horrible journey of thirst and heat—and exhaustion. What a remarkable transformation right here in Gigi's living room." Isabella looked pleased.

"You met then," Gigi said.

"I came for a bath, as you can see," his sister answered, "and here was Corrine. We startled each other half to death, didn't we?"

"I've never seen you act before," Gigi commented to Corrine. "You've never even talked about it."

Corrine shrugged. "Your sister understands."

"I am surrounded by show business," Gigi teased. "Should we go somewhere to celebrate?" It was the first time he'd seen Corrine even remotely sociable.

They walked a few blocks to a French bistro on Thirty-Fourth Street with white tablecloths and soft lighting. Corrine inspected the menu, while Gigi and his sister chatted. When the waiter came, Corrine asked him something in French, he nodded an eager answer and she ordered prune-stuffed pork loin. Isabella found that intriguing enough to order the same, then she smiled her winning stage smile. "So," Isabella said, "here we are."

"Do you know people?" Corrine blurted.

"Well, of course, dear. I know lots of people. I've been in New York for ten years. My word, Gigi, has it been ten years?"

"Can those people help you?"

Isabella glanced over at Gigi before answering Corrine. "You mean with my singing? Well I suppose some have. They might give me information about what's coming or who might like my kind of singing. That's happened. I've had my moments, of course." At this, she smiled again.

But Corrine did not smile. She bit at her lower lip and watched Isabella closely. "How do you know who will lead you somewhere?"

"Oh well, that's a question. I suppose you don't. I just make friends and one thing leads to another. Teachers can lead you somewhere. They have their connections and their ways. If you're a favorite— things can happen."

"I see," Corrine said, but her tone said she clearly did not see.

"Don't worry, dear. Things happen. You're studying your Method. You crossed the great desert for me. Something will happen."

"You've already been here ten years," Corrine challenged.

"I know. And I've had some very nice opportunities in small clubs. I was in the chorus on Broadway for *The Boy Friend*, just before it closed. That was a thrill, really. Just to be there for a few weeks. But I'm not much of a dancer, that's my problem with Broadway." She looked at her brother. "Natty thinks I have an astigmatism. Why else would I be so clumsy?"

Gigi said to Corrine, "Our dad used to tease her about tripping on the flowers in the carpet." Both brother and sister laughed at this memory, but Corrine did not join in. Then the food arrived. Corrine shifted her focus to the pork loin and said little more.

Just as they had agreed to split a crepe for dessert, Isabella asked, "Where did you grow up, Corrine?" Corrine pretended not to hear. Isabella went on. "I suppose Gigi's told you a hundred stories about our little town in Northern Minnesota. Oh, Gigi, I forgot to tell you. A boy who grew up in our town is playing here in the Village. Folky-type songs. He kind of shrieks, I heard."

"You're kidding. I think I heard him. He's from back home? Why would he sing about trains?" Gigi shook his head.

"But people like him. He'll probably be famous before I am."

"Who will be famous?" In her concentration on the last bits of her meal, Corrine had missed their conversation about the singer.

"A boy who grew up in our town," Isabella said and smiled again. She knew so well how to be gracious.

"What did he do to be famous?"

"Well, he's not famous yet," Isabella explained. "But he's getting noticed. He sings folk music."

"The guy at the Gaslight who can't carry a tune," Gigi threw in.

"Bob Dylan," Corrine said. "He's going to be famous because he's different." She gave Gigi a knowing look.

"Well, good for him," Isabella concluded and sipped her coffee.

"My mother's from Paris," Corrine said suddenly. "That's how I'm different. This restaurant reminds me of places I used to go with her."

"Is she still alive, your mother?"

"Oh," Corrine looked surprised. "She is."

"Do you see her?" Isabella asked.

Corrine pushed her wayward curls behind her ears. "It's complicated, I suppose." She met their eyes. "Many things are complicated."

Later, Gigi left Corrine in the apartment to walk his sister to the subway entrance. "Where did she come from?" Isabella asked. "In your life, I mean. Where did you meet her?"

"At Billy Jo's Valentine's party."

"And she's living with you already? It isn't even Easter."

"You think I should have waited for another holiday?"

Isabella ignored his joke. "Where did she live before she came to your apartment? With her mother?"

"I don't know."

"She doesn't talk about herself?"

"Never."

"Goodness, Gigi, people have to belong somewhere. They have to be attached somewhere. That's how we know who we are."

"I suppose."

She kissed his cheek as she headed down the subway stairs. "Get her story. Thanks for the bath."

When he returned to the apartment, Corrine came out of the bathroom wearing only her yellow, fringed scarf and looking so much like his old dreams of her that he caught his breath. She threw herself at him with interest and real feeling, he thought, though he didn't want to think. He wanted to give in to her, this mysterious, unpredictable girl. She took a deep breath like he'd seen her do as she finished crossing the desert. "Are you acting?" he said into her ear. "Are you practicing on me?"

"I am," she whispered. But Gigi did not believe her. He found her lovely and true. And he had difficulty leaving her the next morning, her arms and legs stretched so easily across the bed, one foot poking out from the sheets, her crazy hair. They'd crossed a threshold, he and Corrine. They were lovers now. They could live together forever as far as he was concerned, roll together each night, make plans, follow dreams, grow violets.

Gigi walked to work dazed that he could have nurtured a dream like Corrine and have that dream come true. Here in New York City. Where the street sweeper coming along Seventy-Third Street waved to him from the cab of the sweeper and the Hungarian baker called to him from the doorway of his store and his own spot awaited him behind his counter at the jewelry store.

He worked all day in a deep contentment. One of the store clerks teased him about his dreaminess. "A young man's fancy, Giovanni," she said several times during the day, raising an eyebrow strategically. He didn't hear when the French woman came into the store and asked to have her locket repaired. He'd hardly noticed anyone all day. Then she stood in front of him, small and pretty, and handed him a locket on a gold chain, the locket engraved, the kind of keepsake he saw often and enjoyed fixing, knowing the piece would live long, be passed along from one girl in the family to the next.

"It's the clasp," the woman said, her accent light, but distinguishable. "It will not keep. Or stay." She smiled at her own loss of words and shook her head as if to make the sentence right.

Gigi took the locket from her and studied the problem. "I will need to replace it," he said.

"In gold?"

"Of course," he reassured, "just like this one. You won't know the difference. It's a beautiful necklace," he added, as he often did, to let his customers know he understood how much these trinkets meant in their lives.

"You are so kind," the woman answered as Gigi filled out the order slip. She left then, and Gigi slipped the locket into an envelope with the order slip taped to it. It was Friday afternoon; he would not get to it until the next week.

All weekend he and Corrine relaxed together. On Saturday night he convinced her to leave the house and walk with him. Without thinking or planning it, Gigi led them to the bar where he'd first seen her. "Should we go in?" he asked. She shrugged, but said nothing. Once inside, Gigi looked for signs that she might be known there, but it did not seem to be so. A different bartender poured drinks. Nobody acted as though she had once been a regular, and they drank their beers in complete anonymity.

"When I met you at Billy Jo's party and said I knew you, it's because I saw you here," Gigi ventured, "at that table by the door. And I wanted to know you, but you left too soon. I couldn't find you again." He watched closely as he said all this.

"But you did find me," she said.

Gigi wanted to go on with his story of how he had searched for her, returned to this bar many times thinking she'd come back. He wanted her to know his heart and how much she meant to him. But Corrine had answered him without expression. Instead of looking into his eyes, she dug for the occasional cigarette she liked to smoke and studied the other patrons of the bar. Perhaps it was another performance. She had told him days earlier that she loved smoking, that tapping and lighting and handling a cigarette created an aura of sophistication and separation. Why would you want to be separate, he'd asked. We're already separate, she said. Smoking only makes it more bearable.

After Corrine finished her cigarette, they walked back to the apartment not talking. Gigi had become used to not talking with Corrine. She kept apace, hummed a song he didn't recognize, one of those folk songs maybe or something from her French childhood. He didn't ask. He felt pleased enough just to be going home with her to a space they shared. "You're perfect," he said to her later in bed, realizing instantly that this was a lie, but he liked how the words made him feel, like a man who knew women, like a man who understood perfection.

"I am?"

"You're perfect," he lied again.

Monday morning he went to work in the same cloud he'd been in since the Friday before. He let the clerks tease him as he set out his tools, adjusted his lamp, and started his first job for the day. Just before closing, with only a half hour left, he took out the pretty French woman's locket to fix its clasp. After the quick repair, he polished away the fingerprints and then, because it was too late to start another project and almost time to go home, he opened the locket to see what had been captured inside. An engraved rose decorated its cover and inside he found a picture of Corrine, a younger more tidy version, but surely Corrine, with her curls and fair skin, looking serious, he thought, and older than her years.

The name Gigi had written on the order slip was Claire Bernard. He took a scrap of paper and copied her name and phone number down for himself, then folded it into his wallet. He put away his tools, left the repaired locket with the other completed orders in the wooden box at the front counter, and walked home thinking about the small, polite woman who might be Corrine's mother, the French mother she was sometimes willing to mention. Did this mother know her daughter was living with him, that she roamed the streets of New York alone at night and wanted to be an actress? Did she know anything about the daughter whose photo she carried inside the gold, engraved locket?

Suddenly Gigi could not get back to his apartment fast enough. Whatever he thought he knew about Corrine was so thin, scraps of tissue, really, easily torn and blown away. He walked faster, almost loping through the rush-hour traffic along Madison, over to Park, and into Midtown. At his corner he stopped to buy a bunch of roses, hot pink and full like the one engraved on the locket. "He's in love, yes?" the older lady at his market asked with the same knowing tone as the clerks in the jewelry store. "He buys roses for love, yes?"

He climbed the stairs two at a time and rushed into the apartment calling her name, knowing instinctively what he would find. He'd known it since he left the jewelry store. She was gone. Now that he had one sure piece about her, the photo in a round gold locket belonging to Claire Bernard, who came into the Upper East Side jeweler and presented him with her broken clasp, now that he had that, almost something, he came home to find he had nothing. Corrine was gone.

Her few possessions were gone as well. Frantically he paced the two rooms hunting for a sign or a note, anything to explain why she would leave when they were doing so well. She'd cleaned the sink and watered the violet. She'd left no towels scattered in the bathroom and no records stacked on the phonograph. But these considerations did not explain anything to Gigi. For the first time since his father died, he sat on the sofa and cried, a cry that started in sadness and ended in a lonely plea. He so wanted this girl to love him. In his obsession and imprudence, he could not let go. He knew he was foolish. His sister and Billy Jo certainly thought he was. But their concerns only fortified his desire.

The apartment grew dark. Gigi finally collected himself and turned on a light, trimmed the ends off the roses, and put them in an empty jar with water, which he placed on the table by his bed. Then he went out to search. He stopped by the bar they'd visited Saturday night and poked his head into the French restaurant where they'd eaten with Isabella. He splurged on a cab ride back to the Gaslight, which made him feel even worse. It was a symbol of Corrine's elusiveness. He hadn't been able to claim her there, and the Gaslight's folk music and poetry never spoke to him or eased his aching. But Corrine was not at any of the places where Gigi went. He returned home and went to bed, his mind still racing.

He needed to keep unearthing real facts—numbers and places, the people in her life—then maybe he'd understand why she wandered alone and had a black eye and seemed so disconnected from everyone. He could find where Claire Bernard lived. He was certain he could. And she would connect him to Corrine.

After a restless night alone in his bed for the first time in almost two weeks, he got up early and reached the jewelry store by eight, let himself inside, and moved quickly to retrieve the envelope with the locket that he had left for Mrs. Bernard. He sat at the jewelry counter and called her.

"Hello?"

"Mrs. Bernard. This is Gigi Paulo calling from the jewelry store. Your locket is ready, and I thought if you gave me your address, I could have it delivered to you."

"Oh," she laughed girlishly in response, as though this young jewelry repairman was flirting with her. "I'm sure there is no need. I can be by someday soon. It looks good?"

Gigi wanted her to come that day. He could take his break, follow her home, and learn where she lived and where Corrine must also live and he'd learn all this today, in only hours and then he'd know something. "You must see how good it looks," he urged. "Come by today and say hello."

"Oh goodness," she said. "We'll see." And she laughed again, in French he thought, with the same lilt as her words had. Then she hung up.

For two days Gigi worked on edge waiting for her to come by for her locket and lived equally on edge at home waiting to hear Corrine's knock at his door. The pink roses he'd bought for her opened large, reminding him of his mother's peonies that blossomed every June in the bushes along the house, ants crawling out of them and onto the tables. He'd wanted the roses to make Corrine happy, so she'd stay with him and tell him her secrets, love him the way he loved her.

Corrine was the only want Gigi remembered having. He'd grown up content and learned his father's jewelry repair trade without considering other options. He was not the type to strive for a car, a house, work with status. He'd always wanted love and good living, and he'd had that. When he was a child, his mother kept a companionable household, a prolific garden, a sense that they had everything reasonable beings could dream of having. Every Friday she baked bread, and the aroma of the yeast would waft through their small house. Occasionally she would cut hunks of the dough and drop them in hot oil to fry, and they'd eat sweet substantial bread donuts for lunch. That was the life that had shaped him. He'd never wanted more until he saw Corrine. Now this want for her compelled him to run ragged, step beyond himself, and call customers when it wasn't his place to do so.

Gigi hurried to work Friday morning, certain that this was the day Mrs. Bernard would come for her locket. She'd said she'd stop by this week, and today was the last day. Crossing the many streets along Madison Avenue, he fantasized how he would greet her, maybe even comment on the locket, maybe ask if that was her daughter's photo, what a lovely girl. And maybe Mrs. Bernard would laugh at that, her tickle of a French laugh, and say oh no her daughter was not a girl anymore, but a young woman. Then maybe Gigi could say you must miss her, as though the daughter lived far away, simply a polite guess in the pitter-patter of small talk. And Mrs. Bernard would say but she does not live far away. And she'd smile. And still he'd know nothing. That was why he needed to follow Mrs. Bernard home to a real address, to a real piece of information.

He came into the store and went immediately to the wooden box of repaired items, each in its own envelope ready to be claimed and paid for by the owner, but he could not find Mrs. Bernard's envelope. It was not there. Gigi opened and closed the jewelry counter drawers in a kind of terror. How could it be gone? What could have happened? He called out to his colleague, Bernice, who was unpacking an order behind a far counter. "The Bernard woman's necklace—it's not here. I thought she'd be in today."

"Bernard? Oh, the little French lady. She came by just as I was locking the door last night. So pretty. All in a rush."

"And she left with it?"

Bernice gave him one of her maternal smiles. "Of course, Gigi. What else would she do?"

"I had a question to ask her."

"Call her then. We still have her number on the receipt."

Gigi straightened in excitement. "Do we have her address on file too?"

Bernice sashayed across the store to a file drawer, unlocked it with one of the tiny keys hanging on a chain around her neck, and flipped through the files, her long fingernails clicking as she searched. "No address," she answered. "Sorry." She turned away from him and went back to work. The locket was gone. He no longer had a plan. He no longer knew what he had.

April in New York brought bursts of tulips and daffodils. Fruit trees blossomed, all the trees in Central Park popped tiny green leaves, and people came outside in droves, it seemed to Gigi. Spring in New York happened, an event of color, excitement, and chatter. Every little bird flitting from here to there building a nest had something to chirp about from the minute the sun rose until it set in late evening. Gigi took to walking home along Fifth Avenue. Alone and lonely, he dallied, ate hot dogs on the street for dinner, stopped occasionally in a Midtown bar or movie theater.

Billy Jo called one night to see what on earth he'd been doing, he was never home, she'd even come by once after a tap class. Then she scolded him again for his unrelenting fascination with Corrine, which anyone could see was ruining his life. "The problem is that Method acting she's into," Billy Jo concluded. "It's dark, Gigi. I told you."

"That has nothing to do with it, Billy Jo. She has some secret, something she's hiding that I think makes it hard for her to be with people."

"My friend Jeannie's still interested in you. Why don't you take her to a show or something? You never know."

"I can't," he said.

"Then let's go to Chinatown and eat for cheap. Tomorrow."

"I can't," he said again. "Some other time."

"Darn you," Billy Jo said before she hung up.

Then Isabella called. "I have such news, Gigi. I've met my match, the man for me. And he adores me so." His sister had been married once, to a waiter with large dreams. But that was years ago now, a mistake she never even discussed. "We're having a gathering at his place, a true soiree with all our friends. So they can meet each other. You must come. Bring that interesting girl if you like, but you must come, Gigi. Next Friday." She went on about her man, Monti, who knew everyone in New York, produced acts all over town and was brilliant, brilliant. She said she must run now because they were off to see *Carnival!*, which of course she would rather star in than watch, but one had to keep moving forward, that was the thing.

Isabella believed in moving forward. She'd left home at eighteen, come to New York on her own, and was still moving forward ten years later. She'd sung for weddings and funerals. She'd done short runs in small clubs and gained a loyal following that loved her rich voice and hesitancy on stage, her seeming disbelief that such a sound truly belonged to her. Isabella didn't complain that her moment had not yet come. It was coming, she knew. If she could get a leading role or cut a record, her moment would happen. It took so little really, she told Gigi. Just one wonderful bit of luck. She always assumed it was just around the corner, that one more turn would do it. So she sold hats at Bonwit Teller and sang her songs and moved forward.

A week later Gigi made his way to a roomy apartment on the Upper West Side, with parquet floors and a bay window looking out over the back alley and fire escape. Isabella's new man, Monti, greeted Gigi at the door, black hair smoothed back and brown eyes eager behind his glasses. "Isabella's brother? Heh, what a family. Glad to meet you. Glad you came." He pumped Gigi's hand and slapped his shoulder all at the same time. Then he turned to greet another guest before Gigi could even respond.

Gigi found a spot on the sofa near the bay window and settled himself. Spotting him, Isabella brought a glass of wine and perched on the arm of the sofa next to him. "Isn't he just Mr. New York," she said, her eyes on Monti as he pumped a few more arms. "I truly adore him. And he truly adores me too." She frowned. "Where's your girl, Corrine?"

"I have no idea." He drank his wine, looking straight into his sister's eyes, which clouded for only a moment.

"She'll be back." Isabella grinned. The game of love made sense to her just now, all hope and happy endings. "You'll see. Do you know anyone here?" She searched the room on Gigi's behalf.

"It's fine, Bella. I'm happy here."

She kissed his cheek with a dramatic flourish and went off to stand by her man, Monti. Gigi did not get bored at these New York theater parties that Billy Jo and Isabella loved to throw. He never saw one single person that he would ever have encountered in Northern Minnesota. New Yorkers loved their affects, their cocked heads and wide stances, tossed curls, nervous hands, grand gestures. He was pretty sure that most of them assumed an audience at any moment. Someone's eyes were always watching. Fate hovered. It had to—this was New York.

Isabella's man, Monti, however, did not act as though he were on stage. Rather he acted as though he ran the theater. Monti was a man in charge. He had gathered a group of middle-aged cohorts, all standing near the makeshift bar across the room, all the type to be in charge. Gigi studied these men as they laughed loudly at one another's comments and leaned in tightly when someone in the group spoke more seriously, perhaps confidentially. He wondered what it was they were saying. Were they exchanging financial tips, political opinions, where to get their suits pressed? He couldn't imagine. He watched Monti and his friends as a detached outsider. He did not know their world or even want to.

As Gigi watched from across the room, one of the men turned his focus from the group to look right at him. It startled Gigi, this unexpected connection from a stranger. The man's blue eyes startled him as well, for they were even more blue than his own or Isabella's, the frosty blue of a winter's sky. Gigi held his breath. The man's gaze had pulled Gigi from the crowd in the room and bound him to the stranger, so that Gigi no longer even heard the party around him. And then the man sneered. Or was Gigi imagining this? No, the blue-eyed man fixed a sneer on Gigi, who had never even seen him before, who did not know him from any other successful-looking man on the street. Gigi didn't understand and felt all the strength in his body recede as he held on in confusion and alarm. The man wanted to communicate something to Gigi, a threat or boundary of some kind. Or was it a challenge? Was this total stranger posing a challenge to Gigi?

For an instant he thought he should look behind him. Maybe a menace lurked out on the fire escape. But he knew this was not so, for the stranger's blue eyes had focused on him, nobody else. And then it was over. The man laughed easily at something Monti said, took a sip from his drink, and let go of Gigi completely. He let go of Gigi so completely, that the whole incident seemed not to have happened. Except that it did, and Gigi's shaky hands and weakened legs remained testament.

For the rest of the evening, Gigi did not move from the corner of the sofa. He continued to clutch his glass as the other partygoers mingled around him, told their stories, drank too much and, finally, departed. Monti came over to Gigi at sometime during the evening and slapped him on the back with a "Heh, Giovanni," then moved on again. Monti's blue-eyed friend never gave Gigi another glance, but he stayed until only a half-dozen people remained. By this time he was sitting at the dining table, his back to Gigi, talking with another of Monti's friends, both of them smoking cigars that filled the apartment with thick and powerful fumes.

When Isabella came near, he asked her to sit for a minute. "Who is the man at the table, in the white shirt, dark hair, with his back to me? How does your man Monti know him?" He put his index finger to his lips to signal that she must whisper.

"I'll ask," is all she said. "I'll tell you tomorrow." Before she flitted off again, she added, "Isn't he too wonderful?"

"You mean Monti?"

"Who else?" she answered.

Gigi stayed close to the phone all morning waiting for his sister's call, but instead, she came to his door. "So the man with the black hair who was sitting at the table is Monti's friend from his club. His name is Charles Bernard."

"Bernard."

"Charles Bernard."

"Bernard," Gigi repeated.

"You think you know him or something?" she asked. Gigi could only say no, that he was simply curious because the man seemed to recognize him. "But you didn't talk to him? You didn't ask?" Isabella looked incredulous. "Why wouldn't you just ask, Gigi?"

"A woman came into the jewelry store to have me fix the clasp on her locket. Her name is Bernard."

"What a coincidence! It's such a small world, isn't it? Even in New York. But why would he know you? Did he come into the jewelry store too?"

"No, but there was a picture in the locket."

"Of Charles Bernard?"

"No, Bella, please concentrate on my story. The picture in the locket was of Corrine. As a girl. Maybe a thirteen- or fourteen-year-old girl, but certainly Corrine."

"My word, this is all too much. You think they're related?"

Gigi nodded. "I think Corrine is their daughter."

"My word, but why would he recognize you?"

"He already knew who I was. He must know I'm connected to Corrine. Maybe he's the reason she went away."

"Goodness, Gigi, you are getting much too dramatic here. It's not like you. Maybe you look like someone else he knows, or maybe you misunderstood his expression. That can happen, Gigi. People misinterpret. You know that's true."

But Gigi knew that in this case, it was not true. He didn't know exactly what was true, but when he remembered Charles Bernard's look across Monti's living room, Gigi knew it was some kind of challenge. He had not misinterpreted that.

"I got to run, Gigi. Monti's taking me to Elaine's tonight to introduce me to a producer—he might need a singer for his show." She shivered in her excitement. "I can't believe this is happening to me."

"Maybe you could find out where the Bernard family lives for me, Bella. Monti must know. Don't tell him why, but I think it would help me find Corrine."

His sister studied him for a minute before she said, "Monti knows everything. If you're sure you really want to know."

"I want to find Corrine."

"Oh dear. What will come of this I cannot say," Isabella said, then she sighed and left.

∽

When he hadn't heard from her by midweek, he called. "Did Monti give you the address?"

"Gigi, I'm sorry I didn't call. It's been the worst week."

"So he didn't know?" Gigi could not believe he was pressing his sister in this way when she sounded so distressed.

"Monti and I had a fight. Already when we're supposed to be in love. He didn't like the dress I wore to Elaine's. He said I was stuck. Why didn't I dress like Audrey Hepburn, then maybe I'd get somewhere? I don't know. It was awful."

"Was he drunk?"

"Of course." She started to cry.

"You don't need his type to make it in music."

"His type?"

"Like his friends at the party. Like that Charles Bernard, slick types."

"Is that what you thought of Monti?" She'd stopped crying.

"I didn't take to that group of men too much, Bella. Overall. But I didn't really talk to Monti."

"I wanted him to get to know you. You're my brother. I just thought he adored me. I really did. Audrey Hepburn. She can't even sing."

"He didn't know where Bernard lives?"

"This girl's going to be the end of you, Gigi. Monti said Charles lives on Fifth Avenue, past the museum. Monti says he's rich. That's what he said and I didn't ask more. It was the night he didn't like my dress."

Gigi considered the information about Charles Bernard. "But I thought Corrine was poor. She's always so raggedy."

"Rich people don't have to look nice if they don't want to. She's just expressing herself. It doesn't mean she couldn't be dressed to the hilt. Or like Audrey Hepburn," she added.

"I suppose," he agreed, but for him the pieces did not fit.

The next month felt unbearable to Gigi in spite of the season. A new flock of girls dropped by the shop to see him, referred by Billy Jo and his sister, he was sure, all of them so worried about their charm bracelets and delicate earrings with one or two fake stones missing. They told him their names, the last little part they'd landed at the 54th Street Theater, the Lyceum or such. They complimented his work, asked him how he liked New York, had he seen *The Fantasticks* yet or *Camelot*. He wished them well in his sincere way and he hoped they believed him, although he no longer believed himself. He was not at all sure their dreams would come true, any more than his own would. Just because New York City had mesmerized them didn't mean it would embrace them.

"Gigi, you are a magnet for these girls," Bernice commented, peering at him over her reading glasses. "But none is the girl for you, eh? The girl for you does not show up. Her bracelet is not broken." She shrugged in sympathy.

Then on a blustery day in early June he left the jewelry store to find Corrine waiting for him outside the Hungarian bakeshop down the block, eating little cookies out of a bag. "Hello," she said as though there had been no separation. "Nice tie."

Stunned, he merely said, "My sister bought it for me."

"Nice sister. You want one?" She offered the bag of cookies. He couldn't think. After all these weeks, she was right in front of him offering cookies. He didn't know what it meant. "I'll walk with you," she said.

"It might rain." He glanced at the rolling gray clouds. It took him a full block before he asked, "Where have you been?" His voice did not sound right, even to him.

"Let's go to that bistro where we went with your sister." She smiled, a pretty smile he hardly knew.

"You're happy?" Gigi asked, because there she was in a light green skirt and sweater, with only one scarf around her neck, tied in a bow under her chin. She did not look like the Corrine of early spring. Her hair remained wild, but it was shorter, trimmed. "You look happy."

She did not answer. She ate her cookies and walked on, dodging other pedestrians as she went. Just before they reached the restaurant, the rain started, sudden and hard, so that girls on the street squealed and ran for cover. Gigi saw men put their newspapers over their heads and street vendors scramble to cover their food. But Corrine kept going as though there was no weather, no giddy hysteria, just herself and her companion walking in rhythm down Park Avenue. They entered the bistro with rain dripping off of them.

Gigi immediately ordered a bottle of wine. Corrine took in the restaurant as she had that night so many weeks ago with Isabella. "This is where I want to be," she said. "So comfortable and so French." The waiter brought the wine, opened the bottle, and poured. Then he went over special items on the menu—a soufflé, some type of roast. The man's words blurred as Gigi watched Corrine concentrate and make her choice, as if the food order held great import, could determine an outcome that mattered to her. In the end she selected an asparagus omelet. Gigi ordered the special roast, not sure or caring what that would be. When the waiter left, he leaned across the table. "Where did you go? Why did you leave?"

"It was nothing." She shrugged.

"I want to know where you live—in case something happens."

She almost smiled. "What do you think will happen?"

"I could get sick. I could have an emergency. And you wouldn't know. I wouldn't be able to reach you."

She shrugged again. "It's nothing. You will not get sick or have an emergency. Look at you, Gigi. All is well. You are always well."

"I am not. I don't even know your full name or where you live or why you left me. How can I be well?"

"You used to be, I think." The waiter brought bread, and she began an involved business of cutting slabs of the butter and arranging them on her bread. "Your red table." She looked up at him. "Nobody who is not well has a red table." She said this knowingly, then went back to her bread.

"Please tell me why you went. Without even saying."

She glanced around the restaurant to make sure nobody was paying any attention to them, then pushed up the sleeves of her sweater to reveal dark bruises around her arms, where someone had squeezed too hard and too long. "Things happen, Gigi," she said, her eyes on his.

"Who did this?" He shook his head to throw off what he had just seen. Then it hit him. "Charles Bernard," he said so quietly, she heard only because she already knew. "He's your father, isn't he? He does this to you."

Corrine had looked up to show him her bruises, but now she went back to eating her bread and butter. She did not talk until after the waiter had brought their food and after she'd taken several bites of her omelet and licked her lips. "Did your sisters sing at home?" she asked then, not seeming to notice his misery.

"All my sisters sing," he answered.

"Not all families sing, Gigi. Did you know that? Would you mind if I ordered a crème caramel?"

He didn't answer. He didn't even know what it was that she was ordering and didn't talk while she ate it, but his mind raced away to the days when his sisters sang, when he and his father fished, when he thought he would marry a sweet girl like his mother and live there in town and carry on his father's repair business. He raced back again to New York earlier that spring, in a new year with a new young president and streets teeming with possibility and the girl he loved staying with him. He dashed between the times that had been his and this small table on Thirty-Fourth Street, where Corrine ate custard and caramel in tidy bites off her spoon and the waiter came by to refill his glass and a June storm raged outside.

"Marry me," he said.

She did not answer, but continued eating until there was no food left on any of her plates, not even the butter. Then she said, "I do not have a father. Charles Bernard is not my father. My father died—in the war my mother said, and maybe this is so. But I think he left. In war, men do whatever they want and who asks? Babies are born, girls misused, whole towns burned and what can anyone say? It is war. There are two sides of the story, maybe more."

"Then who is Charles Bernard?"

She wiped at her mouth with her napkin. "You do not want to know."

"I do."

"It is complicated. Nobody sings, Gigi, like I said. Do you understand?"

"No, I don't. I don't understand anything here. Charles or the bruises, the woman Claire who comes into the shop. Who is Claire?"

"She's my mother's friend. My mother is in Paris still. She has a husband now, not so smart, but good. He is good at least. He stays."

"And Claire's her friend?" He said this to urge her on, to learn more, get more pieces, try to understand whatever he could about her.

"Claire is my mother's friend and Charles is Claire's brother. Her younger brother. When he came to America to get rich, she followed him. She thinks she looks after him, but that is impossible, of course. He is the boss. What can she say?"

"Why do they matter to you?" Gigi reached his hands across the table for hers, but she kept her hands under the table in her lap. "Marry me," he said again. She continued to stare at the other side of the restaurant.

"You had a nice house in Minnesota, didn't you? Your sister Isabella, she's nice. You're nice. Everywhere you had those thousands of lakes. Pretty lakes. Your mother grew flowers, I suppose." She pulled on her pale green bow to center it just under her chin. "See? My life, Charles, whatever goes on in my life, you could not know, Gigi. You cannot know."

He didn't like anything she said. "How is Charles rich?" he asked to get her back into her story.

"International business, he says. Foreign trade." She shook her short curls. "He is probably a crook."

"And you all live together?"

"I might have more water, please," she said to the waiter and stared at her empty glass until it was full again. She drank the entire glass in large swallows without a pause, then set the glass back onto the table and dabbed her mouth with the white cloth napkin. "I can stay with you, if you want."

He took in her small face and fragile body. Watching people had always led him to answers, but Corrine revealed nothing that was important. Whatever he thought he knew shifted each time he encountered her. Gigi's heavy heart kept him from saying more.

When they stepped outside the restaurant, a gust of wind caught them off guard, tossing Corrine against Gigi. She laughed wildly as they walked the short blocks to Gigi's apartment then fell onto his bed, the summer storm raging and noisy at the windows. Corrine's battered, thin arms wrapped around Gigi and he held on, rescued for at least that night. He had her in his grasp this moment. Beyond that he had no thought.

⧼⧽

The morning after glistened, the rain gone and the air clean. Gigi opened his eyes to Corrine's face next to him and her pale green clothes on the floor. "I can stay, if you want," she said, just as she had the night before. "For today, anyway. Maybe tomorrow."

"I think you should stay here permanently," he answered.

"It's a nice day. After the rain." She climbed over him to retrieve her clothes. Dressed, she ran her fingers through her messy hair and went into the bathroom. Gigi called in sick to the jewelry store, something he had never done, and they took up their day together. Corrine would not talk about her situation. She would not respond to his appeals. She wanted only one turn to follow the next, and so it went for three days, from breakfasts at the bright red table to late nights in Gigi's bed. Corrine stretched and puttered and napped like a cat in a courtyard. Through all this, he functioned in a daze, not going to work, not talking to anyone but Corrine, barely eating.

Even as he touched the smooth skin on her face, he knew he had lost. And still he held on. He loved her every elusive gesture and mysterious silence. He couldn't help himself.

One afternoon they went to Battery Park to ride the ferry. She hadn't been on the ferry to Staten Island before, not that she could remember. Gigi told her that he took the ride several times a year just to be on a boat, just to be on water. He told her how he and his father had fished the lakes near his home, sometimes getting out by five in the morning to meet the fish when they were most hungry. She listened without comment.

– 90 –

At some point in the ride Corrine asked, "You didn't come to New York to be famous?"

"Doing jewelry repair?" He had to laugh.

"But lots of people do jobs to get by, when what they really want is fame. Like your sister selling hats."

"You think my sister wants fame?"

"What do you think she wants?"

"She wants to sing. And to sing professionally, she has to get the kind of work that maybe brings fame too. If an audience likes her in one performance, they'll want to hear her in another and some record company will want to record her and so on. I guess fame's just part of it."

Corrine's fingers tapped on the ferry railing impatiently. "And all these singers you love so much, Rosemary Clooney, Lena Horne and all, you don't think they want fame?"

"I think they want to sing, like my sister does. Do you want to act or do you just want fame?"

She looked in his direction, her face tight and fierce. "I want to be famous. Think what it can bring, what it can do. Of course, I want to be famous." She let the breeze off the harbor blow her wild hair wilder.

"I always just want a good dinner," he laughed, trying to be light, but meaning it too.

"We are different then, Gigi." She stared out across the water.

In the middle of the night Corrine, still half asleep, reached for Gigi's hand and held it where she wanted it between her legs, rocking meditatively, arching and writhing, almost as in pain. He was not so very experienced with girls, and her solitary orgasm stunned him. He watched her body's outline in the dark, not sure what he should say or do. But Corrine didn't look his way and then collapsed at some point into sleep. When he woke in the morning, she was muttering softly in sleep, like a satisfied baby animal. He sat on his sofa and waited as she slowly emerged and dressed. "I have to go," she said.

"Now?"

"I have to go now. I'll be back. I'll be back another time." She smiled, but it wasn't genuine. She only wanted to leave his apartment without a fuss. He knew this, but still he said, "Don't go. You don't have to leave," but it was more a statement than a plea.

"Thank you," she replied, her green scarf wrapped around her waist like a ballroom sash, her eyes taking in his apartment in the morning light, but not looking back at him. She shut the door behind her, and he was alone.

For a moment he sat immobilized and then, in an instant, he decided to go after her. He pulled on his shoes and ran, taking the stairs four at a time, hanging on to the railing for dear life, and totally alive with hope. He'd follow her, goddamn it. He'd rescue her once and for all. He crashed out the building door into the neighborhood bustle and sun, scanning in every direction for a wisp of pale green skirt or dark curly hair. Surely he was only a moment behind her. He boarded a northbound bus and stood in the middle searching from side to side all the way to Ninetieth. He exited the bus and continued running until he was back at Eighty-Third, searching as he went, scanning for that bit of pale green that might be her skirt or sash. He found a bench along the park and waited. He could see a block, almost a block, in either direction. His sister had said Charles lived past the museum. Maybe right here, Gigi thought, as he sat watch for the rest of the morning.

When the noonday crowd converged on the Metropolitan Museum steps and a flute player took up a tune, Gigi walked that way. Corrine could be anywhere. The many museum flags snapped in the June breeze, the flute tune went on, the people all around chatted and laughed, because it was a summer day in the city and lunchtime and almost Friday. He bought a hot dog and ate it standing, still scouring the people along Fifth Avenue for Corrine.

Then at some point, the flute player packed his instrument and left, and the crowd dwindled. Gigi stayed awhile longer looking at the sidewalks, the doorways of the enormous apartment buildings to the north and the Stanhope across the street, the cabs stopping along Fifth Avenue, everything that moved and any fragment of pale green. But Corrine did not appear. Finally he walked to the jewelry store for the comfort of someplace known and predictable.

Bernice and her older colleague looked up from a conversation with each other to greet Gigi. "The prodigal repairman," Bernice said, but she smiled with genuine warmth. "We thought you ran off and got married." The two women stood, as they often did, behind the engagement rings, those rows of glittering stones all symbolizing love and possibility. "Not married?" The other clerk countered, and he saw the two exchange looks.

"She disappeared," he said.

"What, Giovanni? In a cloud? It was magic? Poof. What do you mean she disappeared?"

Gigi looked uncomfortably at them both. "I can't explain."

"Maybe you should buy her one of these rings. Make a clear message."

The idea of Corrine accepting a traditional diamond and actually wearing it was enough to make him laugh out loud, except he didn't think he could laugh at anything just now. Bernice patted his hand. "It's okay. Life is not so easy, Giovanni. Not for anyone. Listen to the news and what do you hear? Nothing but trouble. This new president? He's got nothing but trouble. That Russian screaming at him and banging his shoes on the table. Krushchev and his threats." Both women shook their heads. "God forbid we're in a war again. Come back at closing and we'll go to Elio's, Gigi. Have some calamari with us."

But Gigi walked home and stayed there. He sat at his bright red table and waited for the sun to set after the long June day. Then he opened a bottle of Chianti, cheap and easy, and drank it slowly without a thought for what he should do next or where his wayward love would lead him.

As his coworkers had said, the world that summer of 1961 had endless troubles. Martial law in Alabama, Communist alliances in North Korea and Cuba, Adolf Eichmann on trial in Jerusalem. On July 2 Ernest Hemingway killed himself and this news in particular rattled Gigi. He'd read Hemingway's short stories in high school English class, stories of men who fished and knew the woods, men like those Gigi had known growing up. That was years ago, and it wasn't as though Ernest Hemingway was actually in his life, but the death struck Gigi as intimately violent, a gun in his mouth, the early morning, his wife at home, the majestic mountains just there beyond his door. That a man could be so sad or so angry. The news weighed on Gigi for days. It was hard to know what to think. Would the world explode, would the whites kill every Negro in the South, would he himself always be so alone?

He sought out Billy Jo for her optimism. "I told you Corrine would bring you down," Billy Jo said one night when they sat at a neighborhood bar, each sipping beer like it was ten-year port.

"She's gone anyway," he answered, "and this time I don't think she'll be back."

"Of course she will. As soon as you get happy again, Gigi. As soon as you quit moping and take my friend Jeannie to the movies—I hear *Fanny* is good. Maybe you and I should go. But as soon as you're back to being your old charming Gigi again, she'll show up. That's Corrine. She's got some kind of instinct. Like a tiger or something. Like how animals smell things in the air. Is that what they say?"

Good old Billy Jo. He almost laughed. "She's not coming back," he said. "She doesn't love me anyway. A girl in love would stay."

"You never know," Billy Jo argued. "Seems to me girls in love do all kinds of things nobody predicts. They marry men they don't love or run off with the circus or throw themselves in front of trains or join convents. And you have to admit Corrine is not your basic ordinary Billy Jo type of girl." She stared at him long and hard before she said, "I say she'll come around and make you miserable all over again."

August settled over the city, a blanket of smog and humidity. The smell of garbage set out for pickup reeked of discarded onions, fermenting meat waste, banana peels. Gigi hated New York in August. The first summer he lived here, the heat and stench staggered him, that this city he loved could turn on him so. Summers in Northern Minnesota got hot, but remained fresh. One fan in the kitchen window cooled the room even after a full day of his mother's cooking. He'd spent his childhood summers hanging around the lake just outside of town, fishing off the public dock, swimming whenever he felt hot or sticky, swatting deer flies, and pondering the deep forest around him. Northern Minnesota summers had not prepared him for New York in August. His third-floor apartment stayed unbearably hot for weeks. He didn't want to cook. He slept on a sheet in the middle of the floor with a fan aimed straight at him.

"You've got to get out, Gigi," Billy Jo said. "Listen, come watch a show with me tonight. Have a few laughs."

So he went with Billy Jo to a rundown theater off Times Square, where a lineup of performers popped on and off stage—a magic act with birds, a ventriloquist with a five-foot dummy, two balding guys trading barbs about growing up Jewish, punch-line jokes that actually did make Gigi laugh. The last act was a trio of sisters, all dressed in tight red dresses singing a medley of show tunes—"Shall We Dance?" and "Some Enchanted Evening." When they bowed at the end the tiara fell off one of the sisters, and she put it back on at an angle just over her ear.

"I'm as good as those three," Billy Jo commented when they were out of the cool theater and on the street again. "I mean, she couldn't even keep that thing on her head." She sighed. "I would love an act in this kind of show. Like a vaudeville-type show. Maybe I'm not living in the right moment. I'm more of an old-fashioned girl. More of a Rockette type."

"You want to be a Rockette?"

"No, but I mean there's that show business world where girls were supposed to look like me, you know healthy and well-fed."

Gigi laughed. The night's funny bits and easy humor had lifted his spirits.

"Things are changing, Gigi. These kinds of shows, I don't know. I don't think they'll last. Like Charlie Chaplin. Everyone thought he was a genius, but who wants to watch a silent show now? I mean look at *The Fantasticks*. It isn't like old shows, with all the sets and fancy costumes. It's bare. That empty stage. I don't know what I'm really saying. These new things, Gigi, people love them. Things are changing." She shook her head of wavy, set hair with grave concern.

"But we just saw a ventriloquist," Gigi argued. He didn't want Billy Jo to despair. He wanted this one night to end well. "Things won't change too much."

"I hope you're right. Still I'm probably too substantial looking. I should knock off ice cream," she added.

Every hot day that August he came to the jewelry store early and left late, cool in the air-conditioned store and relieved by the work. He'd gone to a flea market with Billy Jo and bought several antique watches, which he hauled out whenever he had nothing else to do, wholly focused on the fixing, thankful not to think.

And then Claire Bernard came into the store again. Bernice had run to the bank and the other clerk was in the back eating her lunch, leaving Gigi the only employee in the store when she entered.

"Hello," she said, clearly remembering him, smiling as an old friend. "You did such nice work on my locket." She fingered it hanging just so around her neck. "Now I have something else." She opened her purse and pulled out a box with the name of a French company imprinted on the lid. She took off the lid and lifted out a silver bracelet with charms, several of which were no longer attached. "I wore it as a child," she explained. "I chose every charm myself." She set the bracelet and its loose charms on the counter in front of Gigi—a star, a swan, the Eiffel tower, a cat with emerald eyes, and the initial C with flowery engraving. She touched them with a certain longing, still smiling politely. "I found it again in my jewelry drawer. Even if I don't wear it, I want it fixed, don't you think?"

Gigi sat frozen. From the minute he'd seen her coming through the door, his mind had been bounding ahead to figure out how he might make this encounter benefit him, how he could make a more lasting connection, get information, find out where the Bernards lived. "They're beautifully made," he said finally, his eyes on the charms. "If you have a few minutes, I can attach the loose charms while you wait. It's a very simple repair." He looked up, trying to seem natural, trying to smile like the old Gigi always did.

"I can wait, yes. Thank you." She set her purse on the floor and leaned lightly against the counter. "I was always so proud to wear my charms. Like a little lady, I used to think."

Gigi bent over the dainty bracelet. "Did the girl in the locket wear this too?" he asked, keeping his voice disinterested.

"Oh," she said, seemingly surprised that he remembered. "No, though that is a good thought. It is wise to keep your sister-in-law happy with little gifts." She laughed her light and untroubled laugh.

Gigi's head jerked up from the repair. "The girl in the locket is your sister-in-law?" His question came like an accusation, landing hard between them. Claire Bernard drew back instinctively, but recovered and laughed again. "Yes, the girl in the locket is my sister-in-law. She is married to my brother."

"But she's a child." Gigi had stopped working on the charms. He stared at Claire Bernard without moving. "She's just a girl."

"Well, it's an old photo of course," she laughed, this time nervously. "But she is young. We've known her forever. Her mother was my best friend from school. In France." She'd recovered from her discomfort with Gigi and continued on with her story. "I am like a godmother. So I sent her a ticket to visit me when she finished school, and my brother fell in love with her. So they married. Such a story, don't you think? C'est la vie." She shrugged and smiled, though Gigi could see something else in her expression. Some apprehension, he thought, some edge.

He nodded automatically and attached the last charm in a daze. "No charge," he said, handing her the bracelet.

"Thank you." She turned to look at him over her shoulder. "Au revoir," she said and walked prettily toward the door and out, knowing he was watching her, maybe even wanting him to watch her. That thought crossed his mind.

He ran back to tell his colleague that he had an emergency and would see her the next morning. He shoved everything into his drawer, unsorted and unordered, locked it, then went out onto Madison Avenue to find Claire Bernard and follow her. She was wearing a simple sky blue dress and matching shoes, her dark hair pulled back with a clip. He found her almost instantly, standing at the window of a lingerie shop, considering something that she saw there. He slowed, fussed with his watch, tried to look like a man who knew what he was doing, like a man who knew where he was going.

He had never in his life behaved the way he had this summer, torturing himself over the figment of a girl, chasing up and down New York streets, wanting and wanting and pushing. "Gigi's always happy, aren't you, dear?" his mother had said so many times. Even in June, Corrine had told him he was well. He was always well, she had said. He'd never stopped to wonder about whether or not he was happy or well. He thought about the world outside of himself—the woods back home, the ingredients for dinner, the giggly girls in front of Macy's, the parts of the watch he was fixing—not his inner workings. His inner workings were to him like breathing and swallowing, like one foot in front of the other, blood flowing, heart pumping, fingers flexing. Things just worked.

Now Gigi had chosen to love someone who had turned him inward. He barely noticed the two elderly men standing nose to nose next to him, arguing in some language he did not know, arms waving at each other, brimmed hats covering their heads in the August heat. Instead he focused on where Claire Bernard might lead him, what he might do when he got there.

Suddenly, Claire moved away from the lingerie window. She turned on Eighty-Third, crossed to Fifth, turned again, and walked briskly to the second building, where she appeared to greet someone coming out before she disappeared inside. Not stopping to think about the consequences, Gigi followed her, opened the heavy door, and stepped into the lobby.

"May I help you, sir?" an older man in a buttoned, gray uniform asked.

Gigi barely hesitated. "I have something for Claire Bernard," he answered, then seeing the doubt in the older man's eyes, Gigi took out his wallet to find one of the jewelry store's thick, cream-colored business cards engraved with his name and occupation. Giovanni Paulo. Fine Jewelry Repair. "She's just been to the shop," Gigi added. "It is important."

"Miss Bernard doesn't live here, you know. She is visiting."

"She's visiting? She's visiting Corrine?"

"You know Mrs. Bernard?" the doorman asked, surprised.

"Of course, of course. I know them, all of them. I know all the Bernards."

The doorman studied the business card in his hand. Then he picked up the phone. "A Mr. Paulo is here to discuss a jewelry matter with Miss Bernard." He listened intently, settled the phone back in its place, and told Gigi that he could take the elevator to the sixth floor.

Gigi thanked him, too fervently, he thought. Still he held his head high as he waited for the elevator. He knew he was, overall, a polished-looking man, always well groomed, and though he bought his shirts off the sale racks, his jacket had been custom made, at his sister's insistence, by a tiny Chinese tailor on Mott Street who spoke no English. Gigi was certain the doorman stood watching his every move, yet as he stepped onto the elevator, he glanced quickly at the desk to find that the older man was back on his phone, tending to some tenant's minute whim, perhaps. The elevator was decorated in mirrors and bronze, the carpet thick and flowered. A single crystal chandelier hung from the high elevator ceiling. This was where Corrine lived. In spite of her bruises and haphazard clothes, she came home to carpet so thick that Gigi could feel it move beneath his shoes. At the sixth floor a subdued bell sounded as the heavy doors opened.

Claire Bernard stood waiting for him, frowning. "You followed me. But I don't live here. I am a few blocks away, you see."

"I wanted to call on Corrine," he said.

"Corrine?" Stunned, she stepped away from him and bumped against the wall. "You know my sister-in-law? You never said you knew her."

"I'm sorry." He stood waiting for Claire Bernard to regain herself, to ask him inside, to find the right balance here. "Perhaps I could say hello," he offered as a possibility.

Claire leaned against the wall next to a graceful table that held a painted lamp and matching ashtray. She took a light hold of the table to support herself, bent toward Gigi and said, "Charles is home." She looked frightened. "It is probably not a good time," she added, still holding the table. "To visit."

The door to the apartment opened so abruptly that both Claire and Gigi drew back. Charles Bernard, though physically dwarfed by the large door and high ceilings, filled the hallway with explosive energy. "What are you doing here?"

"I've come to say hello," Gigi answered.

"What's he doing here?" Charles roared at his sister.

"He fixed my charm bracelet. It's no trouble here, Charles. Really. He's just stopping by." Claire gave a small smile, an effort, but she did not move.

"He's Corrine's lover," Charles said.

Claire Bernard grabbed for the hallway table again. "He is not, Charles! You have gone too far."

Her brother observed her from his stance in the doorway. "No, Claire. I have not gone far enough." He went into the apartment and returned with her pale blue handbag that matched her dress and shoes. "Go home, Claire." He put her fingers around the handle of her bag, physically securing it in her grip, then pressed the elevator button. Doing this seemed to lower his anger, at least at his sister. "This is between Corrine and me," he said. "And this repairman here. This gigolo repairman here."

Claire shook her head as she stepped into the elevator. "You're wrong, Charles. He put all the little charms on my bracelet. Without charge, Charles," she said as the door closed in front of her. "Charles!" they could hear her call one last time.

Neither man spoke. Gigi kept his eyes riveted on Charles Bernard. And Charles stared only at the elevator door that had just closed. Minutes went by and nothing happened. Charles did not look at Gigi, only at the polished door and the flowered carpet in front of it. He had jammed his hands into his pockets, his tie had been loosened earlier, his suit coat removed. He wore gray suspenders attached to his darker gray pants, and he kept his hands deep in the pockets of those pants.

Finally he said, "You will have to decide, repairman." His head snapped in Gigi's direction, but still Gigi waited. "My wife is probably a whore. You are probably one of many." He enunciated every syllable of this word, *probably*, as though he had just learned it and liked its hard sounds. He sneered then the way he had at Monti's party. "She will *probably* give us both some disease and we will die." Charles threw back his head and laughed.

And then she stood in the doorway. Her hair was not loose, but pulled tightly from her face. She wore slacks, narrow and white, and a sleeveless sweater in dark blue or black. Gigi had to concentrate to reconcile the young woman in the doorway with the girl he knew. She had red lipstick on her mouth. Like Billy Jo. She kept her red lips together tightly, frowning, her eyes on Charles.

"Gigi is telling you something funny, Charles?"

"No. I am telling him how we all will die."

"And how is that, Charles? You see, Gigi, how amusing is this little man I married, this little dictator man, so amusing. How are we all going to die, Charles?"

Charles made a low sound, a kind of growl in his throat. "You will die when I kill you. Or you will die alone and poor and nobody will know you. I will die because you are a whore." He'd squared himself in front of her to make this speech, but Corrine did not look afraid or even concerned. Instead she turned to Gigi. "Would you like to come inside? Charles has a lovely apartment here. You should see. But no violet on a table. No violets in prison, is that right, Charles?"

Charles stood between Gigi, who was still near the elevator, and Corrine in the apartment doorway. His skin had become shiny with sweat, a muscle on the left side of his face twitched and, involuntarily, his hands had formed into two tight fists stiff against his legs. In a movement so swift, Gigi did not see it coming, Charles lunged at Corrine and thrust one fist into her stomach then followed that with a hit to her head. She staggered backward with the blows, but made no sound. The cry Gigi heard in the hallway came from his own throat.

He charged to defend Corrine and found himself in a triangular hold, with Charles pushing to get his hands on Corrine's neck and Corrine kicking against Charles and Gigi trying to pull them apart. Gigi could barely see what was happening, they were all so close and all in motion as they tumbled to the floor. But he could smell Charles sweating and Corrine's perfume, the heat off their bodies. Then she wiggled away, rolled over, shoved the heel of her shoe into Charles's neck and broke free to run across the living room. Charles held his throat and remained on the floor.

"Close the fucking door," he roared to Gigi, who did as he was told, then stepped over Charles toward Corrine.

The living room extended wide with windows from the floor to the ceiling, with sofas and chairs in groupings everywhere and lamps and ottomans and ornaments, an obstacle course of lavish furnishings and the afternoon sun. Corrine, her nose bleeding onto her dark sweater and white summer pants, reached for a tall figurine on the shelf over the desk, a ceramic woman in broad white skirts decorated with gold, her swirled white hair also decorated with gold. Corrine gripped it comfortably and walked across to Charles in brisk, even steps, then bent down and slammed the statue against the side of his head. He did not seem to guess what was about to happen to him until the instant Corrine raised the statue over her head. Then he gasped and she struck and his body went limp.

"You see how it is, Gigi," Corrine said, turning away from Charles. "How nobody sings." She pulled the rubber band from her tidy hairdo and shook out her curls. Then she sat down in a deep chair and took in a long, loud breath. "Now you see."

"Is he dead?" Gigi still stood in the middle of the vast room, his blue eyes wide and frightened. "Good Lord, Corrine, did you just kill him?"

She wrinkled her nose at this distasteful notion. "Of course not. You are looking at a man with a very hard head, Gigi. And I am small, of course. Not so strong as his terrible thick head." She smiled as she had when eating crème caramel, he thought. A smile of much contentment.

"We have to call a doctor, Corrine. My God. I just wanted to see you. I thought I'd follow Claire and find you. Now what have I done? What have I caused?" Gigi searched the room for a telephone, but could not identify that one distinct item in this room of everything, of pillows and rugs and art and sun. "Don't you have a phone? My God, Corrine. He may have a concussion. He needs help. Maybe I should get the doorman. He handles problems. He—"

At this suggestion Corrine stood up and came close to him. She put the palms of her hands against his cheeks. "Listen to me, Gigi. This is not your world here. You understand nothing. Charles and I hate each other. It is what we do, how we get by. There is no concussion. There is no doctor or doorman or sister Claire or sweet Gigi with his sad music and cheap wine. This is me and Charles. We do what we do."

"Why did you come to me? Why knock on my door and spend nights with me and come back again?"

She kept her eyes on him and blinked deliberately. "We do what we do." She answered in a tone he'd heard before, concise, without feeling.

"I don't know what that means. You stay married because you hate each other?"

She had stepped slightly away from him and reached for a throw from one of the lush chairs to dab at the blood on her face, a pale woven throw meant to add one more layer of comfort, one more lovely layer, but Corrine used it as a towel and tossed it away on another chair when she was done. She didn't answer his question. "I am going to change clothes," she said. "You can leave if you choose. Or find a chair. Would you like a whiskey?" She tossed all these words out in much the way she'd tossed the bloodied wool throw.

Gigi had no clear thought in his head. Whatever he did next would have to be on instinct, not because he'd thought through the right action. He still searched the room for a telephone, which would at least be a link to the world outside, a world where Corrine had not just left her husband unconscious on the rug and talked about hate the way Charles had talked about killing her, where they had not all skirmished for dear life on the plush carpet. A phone could possibly rescue him. But he did not find a phone, and he did not find a chair, as she had suggested. He stood, himself a statue now, rigid in the middle of the room like no other room he'd ever inhabited anywhere in his life.

His eyes fixed on another tall ceramic figurine high on a shelf, maybe a match to the one Corrine had used to hit Charles, this one with black hair, not white, wearing a pink dress, gilded like the other figurine, even its shoes, he noticed, poking out from beneath the wide, swooping dress. The figurine's tiny painted eyes stared across the room at nothing, not meant to seem real in any way. The tiny black eyes were meant to be just as Gigi saw them—blank, unmoving, and unmoved.

Somewhere else in the apartment, Gigi heard a door slam. The sun shifted on the living room rugs, and he suddenly realized he could hear the traffic on Fifth Avenue faintly, as though miles away. Every few seconds he looked at Charles, who remained as Corrine had left him, maybe unconscious, maybe dead. To leave the apartment Gigi would need to circumvent Charles, then work the lock to the hallway and press the elevator button and hear its bell when the doors opened, and when he arrived in the lobby he'd need to acknowledge the doorman again and act normal, as though he'd just left a normal married couple having whiskeys on the sixth floor.

He glanced around to see what Corrine had done with the white-haired statue. She'd tossed that too, onto one of the very soft sofa cushions, where it lay on its side, oddly crooked because the stiff skirt stuck out inches from the small bodice and head. Even from across the room, Gigi could see the doll's eyes, dots of paint, these in royal blue, gazing out over all the furniture and through the late afternoon light and into nothing.

He had no idea how long it had been since Corrine left the room to change her clothes. He felt his feet move him toward the door, around Charles, and out of the apartment. He did not shut the door behind him or look back or touch anything. When he reached the lobby, the doorman did not look up from his conversation with an elderly lady. Gigi kept his shoulders back as he walked outside the building, but this was not easy for him to do. The weight of something real and terrible wanted to press him down, flatten his soul, and leave him where he could not be found again.

∽

He did not count the weeks. The heat passed, but his apartment held on to summer. Every night in the thick stillness Gigi endured dreams of death and distortion, sneering mouths and painted eyes, blood splattered here and there in oversized rooms that would not allow him to move or escape. If he opened his eyes at two or three in the morning, he would not let them close again, so frightened he was of what waited for him in sleep. He asked his sister if he'd had nightmares as a child, and she'd laughed her musical laugh, such a silly notion. You are not the type, Gigi, she'd said. Corrine came and went in these dreams, but she never spoke to him or touched him or met his eyes straight on. Nor did she wear scarves around her neck or reveal her smooth skin. She came and went in heavy gowns and gold shoes and tossed her hair whenever Gigi called out to her.

The women at work noticed the difference in him, but said nothing. Whatever troubled him, surely it would pass. Young love, it would pass. He curved his shoulders over his work and thought of nothing but the task. He didn't look up when the door opened. He didn't hope for Claire Bernard or Corrine or anyone. He didn't even hope for Billy Jo and her friends, who all expected something kindly from him that he was not now prepared to give. After work he took to getting on a bus to ride out the thirty-some blocks home. And even on the bus he refused to look out the window. He focused instead on a particular within the bus—the rubber matting in the aisle, grosgrain bows on a girl's patent leather shoes, a broken initial on someone's briefcase. Something to hold him. Anything.

Gigi never thought of this time after the Fifth Avenue apartment as a transition or a grieving or a healing. He had witnessed some kind of horror, in his mind. And betrayal. And now he thought he would carry that horror and betrayal forever. He wasn't himself, because that self did not exist anymore. That's what he thought— or more rightly, didn't think. Thought was exactly what he wished to avoid.

He went to the movies at night. He played cards with the family that owned the grocery on his corner. They liked Hearts and Five-card Stud. He threw in his pennies and rarely looked up. He avoided his sister, he put off Billy Jo. Months went by. The Yankees won the World Series. Some Germans escaped East Berlin. French police attacked thousands of protesters in Paris. Fire destroyed Zsa Zsa Gabor's Bel Air mansion. Joseph Stalin's body was removed from the Kremlin and buried elsewhere. All over the world, life continued. Gigi read the headlines. He scanned the dates. When all the leaves dropped from the boulevard trees, he knew that summer was long gone, that winter was on its way. He packed his fan in the back of his closet and pulled out his rubber boots. He did what he did. Just as Corrine and Charles did what they did.

On a Saturday in mid-November his sister called with the news. "You remember that man you asked me about last spring, that Charles Bernard? At Monti's party? He's dead, Gigi! His wife stabbed him to death. On Fifth Avenue. Well, not on the street, in their apartment, but he's dead and they arrested his wife. Didn't you think he might be Corrine's father? You fixed a locket or something? Oh, I'm trying to remember. Do you remember, Gigi? Is this Charles Bernard Corrine's father? Oh God, and her mother arrested. Her father dead and her mother a murderer." Isabella rattled on, beside herself, until Gigi interrupted.

"No Bella, Charles is not Corrine's father. He's Corrine's husband. Corrine is married to Charles Bernard." His voice stayed too flat for the bad news, he could hear that.

"His wife? But she stayed with you. She was your girlfriend. I thought she was, doing her desert walk across your apartment and all. Oh Gigi, this is the worst. She's his wife?"

"I didn't know then, Bella. I didn't know anything."

"What did I say? Didn't I say people have to be from somewhere, attached to someone? I told you, Gigi."

"I know. I think I better hang up now. I better go. Thank you for telling me. I'm sorry you're upset. I'm sorry, Bella." He hung up and noticed the early winter snow, light and delicate, swirling outside his window as in an airy waltz, tiny flakes tilting and rolling as they fell. He stood for a long time at his window watching the snow and hearing his sister's story and her fright and her admonitions over and over in his head. And himself answering that he didn't know.

The next morning he searched the papers for some mention, but found only a small paragraph that the French businessman Charles Christophe Bernard had died at home on Friday, November 17th, and that more details would follow. Two days later the full obituary appeared in the newspapers telling that Charles had been born in Marseille, educated at the Lycée Thiers, and moved to New York in 1946, where he worked in several companies, all listed, all meaningless. He was survived by his wife, Corrine, and sister, Claire. He had died unexpectedly. According to the papers his wife had not stabbed him to death on the sixth floor of their Fifth Avenue apartment amid soft cushions and an array of ornaments as might be found in some small museum. According to the papers he had died unexpectedly.

Gigi thought he had not died unexpectedly at all. Charles Bernard had stood in the hallway next to Gigi and said Corrine would kill them both, though at the time Gigi did not believe him. At the time Gigi had believed the exact opposite, that in a rage Charles would kill Corrine. He would charge at her as Gigi had watched him do, Corrine standing there with her tight mouth and white summer pants and Charles hitting her twice in less than a minute. But then Gigi had seen Corrine crash the figurine into Charles's skull without a qualm and shake out her curls and mop her blood with an elegant throw and think nothing of it. Have a whiskey, she'd said.

Days after the discreet obituary, the story of Charles Bernard's murder hit all the papers and the evening news, a perfect sensation. A wealthy businessman murdered in his Fifth Avenue apartment. His young French wife. The grotesque violence. He'd died of multiple stab wounds from a kitchen carving knife, French with a wooden handle. Only the two of them were home. She said he'd threatened her and she struck to save herself. Eight times, she struck. The news commentators reported in somber tones. Police were investigating.

Two weeks later, a well-dressed man in a gray felt hat showed up at the jewelry store. He asked for Giovanni Paulo. He asked Gigi if they could speak in private. He said he represented the law firm that was defending Mrs. Bernard, who had now been formally accused of killing her husband. She had listed Mr. Paulo as a witness in her favor, a witness who knew of her abusive marriage, her need to protect herself or even strike back. Who understood her vulnerability, as it were. He spoke to Gigi in a composed, informed manner. He assumed Gigi's cooperation. They would like to "run through" his testimony in their offices. Gigi said he could come any day after four. He could leave work and walk to the law offices on Park Avenue. The man gave Gigi his business card and shook his hand firmly. "Good day," he said.

Bernice watched all this from her spot behind the diamond counter. When the door closed and they were alone, she raised her eyebrows, waiting for his explanation.

"He wants me to be a witness."

"I see," she said, but her gaze said otherwise.

"The Bernard murder," he explained, and immediately wished he'd said nothing.

"You're involved?" Bernice shook her head, still looking at him to tell her more.

But he didn't, and he told no one else about the man from the Park Avenue law office. A secretary called him at home to schedule his appointment, and when the day came, he excused himself early from work and went to "run through" his testimony. He had no idea what that really meant. Was Corrine to be on trial? Did they expect him to sit in a witness stand and say she was innocent? He knew nothing of these things other than what he'd seen on the *Perry Mason* television series. The defendant always won. Perry Mason always proved the prosecution wrong. And the innocent thanked him profusely while Della Street smiled her knowing smile.

The law offices were on the first floor of a stone mansion, through double wooden doors on the right of the vestibule. Inside the receptionist seemed to know him and the secretary dressed in the deepest dark brown wool seemed to know him, chatting warmly as she led him to a wood-paneled conference room and poured him coffee the color of her own fitted suit and waited with him until one of the attorneys appeared. The man entered the room with crisp movements and large energy, so that Gigi sat at attention in spite of himself.

"I'm Lafayette Willson, Mr. Paulo. Thank you for coming. As you know, our client, Mrs. Bernard, has been accused of murdering her husband, Charles. In fact she did attack him with a kitchen knife in self-defense. He had hit her many times in the past, as she says you realize, and threatened to strangle her many times, as was the case on the day of his death. We would like to hear what you know about Mr. Bernard's physical abuse of his wife and any other details that could assist us in proving her innocent of first-degree murder."

Gigi stared in wonder. This man had so many words at his disposal and delivered them with such exactness and force, he sounded like he was reading from a script. He really wasn't very different from Perry Mason. While he was talking, the secretary in the deep brown suit had left and two other people had come into the room—one an older woman with a reporting machine and the other a younger man who sat, like Gigi, in rigid concentration.

Lafayette Willson sat down opposite Gigi, nodded to the older woman and asked, "How long have you known Mrs. Bernard?"

Gigi counted quickly in his head and answered that he'd known her ten months. Of course, in his imagination he'd known her for much longer, but they didn't want to hear about that. Even so, the lawyer didn't seem to like his answer.

"And how would you characterize your relationship?"

Gigi answered that they were lovers. Lafayette Willson didn't like that answer either.

"Mrs. Bernard indicated that you were friends, that she visited you several times in the past year and that you had mutual friends, as well. She said you stopped by once recently to visit her. Would you please confirm all of that, Mr. Paulo?"

Gigi said no, they had been lovers, not friends, and that she had stayed with him for days at a time whenever she visited, once for almost two weeks, in fact. And yes, he had visited her in August for less than an hour.

The attorney looked displeased, even concerned. "In those various visits did you ever see that Mrs. Bernard was bruised or showed symptoms of abuse?" Gigi answered that he had seen bruises and went on to tell about the black eye, the marks on her arms, and also the punches to the face that he'd witnessed in her apartment. The older woman typed everything he said. Behind the attorney's questions, Gigi's answers, and the recorder's typing lay a large silence, a significant silence. Not the quiet Gigi knew as he worked on his repairs or the stillness of snow outside his apartment window, but the serious silence of serious doings.

"Did you ever know Mrs. Bernard to defend herself?"

Gigi said that he had seen her fight back. Attorney Willson asked him to elaborate and so Gigi did. He elaborated about Charles saying they'd all die and him lunging at Corrine, the scuffle on the floor with all three of them, and Corrine shoving her heel into her husband's neck, then her careful walk across the living room with the figurine.

"And would you say that she acted in self-defense?"

Gigi stopped. He knew the right answer, the one the attorney wanted to hear. "She was relieved," he said finally. "She sat in a chair to rest."

Willson frowned. "What do you mean by relieved, Mr. Paulo?"

"She asked me if I wanted a whiskey."

The attorney signaled for the recorder to stop. "She hit her husband with a ceramic figurine after he'd punched her twice and caused her nose to bleed. Is that right?"

Gigi nodded.

"Let me ask you again if she acted in self-defense."

"He was already on the floor. She'd already kicked him in the throat with her shoe." Gigi's voice had become slightly frantic in the telling. "She wouldn't let me get help. She took out her ponytail and shook her hair. That's what I mean."

Lafayette Willson pulled himself to an even more stiff and lofty posture. "What exactly do you mean, Mr. Paulo?"

"I mean she'd already defended herself. She didn't need to do more. It wasn't self-defense."

"Then what was it?"

"I think she tried to kill him."

The attorney sucked in his breath and hit the table firmly with his hand. "Well, that's it then, Mr. Paulo. Clearly Mrs. Bernard was wrong in her assessment of your allegiance." He stood up, turned, and left without another word. The younger man and the older woman followed quickly, leaving Gigi alone in the large and serious room. He had not touched his coffee, but now lifted the elegant cup and took a long swallow. In minutes the secretary, who had poured him that coffee and greeted him warmly earlier, came into the room and offered to escort him out.

It was after five by then and dark on the street. For the first time in months, Gigi walked home. Christmas lights decorated the trees and buildings, Salvation Army bells rang out on some corners of Park Avenue, and a deep blue sky covered the city. Walking along the festive blocks through Midtown, he felt just a little better than he had for a long time. He'd hit back. He'd told his story and spoken the truth. If Corrine thought he would lie for her because he had been so in love, then she hadn't ever understood him. He did honest work. He cooked his own food using his mother's methods, he loved his family. He was a man who used to walk out onto the frozen ice and patiently attend to the fish for hours. Whole mornings into whole afternoons waiting for those fish. His father had taught him that and his mother had taught him to cook. His sisters all sang. He didn't need a false lover, a married woman, a murderess.

He bought himself a little steak and went home to fry it in a simmer of onions. Then he ate it with an entire bottle of wine, all the while listening to his beloved sad songs.

∽

On Christmas Eve, Isabella insisted on dragging a small tree up the three flights of stairs to set down next to his sofa near the window. He had colored lights left from the year before, when she had likewise convinced him to get a tree and decorate it. She'd made popcorn chains for the tree on those autumn nights when she didn't perform and Monti didn't show up to keep her company.

"You must have ten yards of these chains," Gigi commented as he wrapped them round and round the little five-foot tree.

"I know," she sighed. "I had to make lots of popcorn." Her relationship with Monti did not seem to be following the course she'd hoped for, though he had found her a club where she now sang on Tuesday and Thursday nights. "It looks pretty though," she said, stepping back to assess their work. "Remember Mama's trees with all the strands of tinsel? What did you do anyway with all those decorations when you sold the house?"

"I packed them. They're in Nat and Bill's garage for now. I had to give so much away."

– 116 –

"To come here." She sounded as though she was responsible. "Poor Gigi."

"I'm all right, Bella. One girl can't ruin me."

But Isabella looked like she believed one girl could. "I guess the trial comes up sometime in February. Monti and his friends from the men's club still can't believe it happened. But he says they never liked Corrine. Not the type to be a businessman's wife, I guess. I told Monti she seemed like a good actress, very focused. Very deep. But he just laughed. She's deep all right, he said. God, I hate insinuation." She rearranged a strand of popcorn and sat down. "Don't you, Gigi?"

"It's a pretty tree," he answered.

When Billy Jo got back in town from spending Christmas with her mother, she phoned Gigi immediately. "Gigi, what can this mean? She's innocent, right? She has to be innocent. I always said she was dark, but I never meant this dark. Stabbing her husband eight times in the middle of the kitchen. That's what I heard, Gigi. Is that what you heard?" She didn't wait for his answer. "Jeannie said she saw Corrine shopping at Bergdorf's for outrageously expensive dresses to wear at the trial, all with matching shoes, Jeannie said, mostly suede shoes, of all the impractical choices, and she hired a Park Avenue law firm to prove it was all in self-defense, that he'd been beating her up for years."

At the end of this rush, Billy Jo lowered her voice and said, "Gigi, did you know she was married? It's okay if you did, because he was a bully, but—I'm thinking is that the reason you were so glum all summer?"

"I didn't know," he answered. "Until August, I didn't know."

"That's what I thought. That you didn't know, because it's just not like you, raised Italian and Catholic and all. Oh, Gigi, I'm sorry I introduced you to Corrine. It's my fault. I should have guessed she was off her rocker from the start, wearing all those scarves and hardly talking and that crazy hair."

"Billy Jo, you think I saw Corrine for the first time at your party, but I'd seen her before. I saw Corrine the first day I got to New York. Before I even walked over to Bella's. Before I met anyone. I went into a bar by Penn Station for a sandwich and there she was. I've thought about Corrine every day that I've lived here." He surprised himself saying this. He spoke without emotion, like he was telling someone else's story, not his own. "She used to come to me in my dreams. And then I saw her at your party."

"Oh my god in heaven, Gigi. Did you tell that to your sister?"

"No."

"Don't."

Gigi fingered the spiky ends of the Christmas tree and waited for Billy Jo to say more on her end of the line. He loved the bright tree lights in his shadowy apartment. He turned them on the second he came home from work and didn't turn them off until he went to bed. Billy Jo lowered her voice, as if someone were listening to everything she had to say. "You and Corrine don't have plans do you? I mean for after the trial? To be together?"

"Actually, Billy Jo, I plan never to see Corrine Bernard again in my life." He meant this, though he hadn't thought it specifically until that moment. Since his appointment at the law office, his dreams of her had come less frequently and less intensely. In his real life he saw no reason that he'd ever have to see her again. He didn't consider whether or not she'd go to jail for her crime. He assumed she wouldn't. He assumed that Lafayette Willson and his colleagues had whatever resources were necessary to persuade a jury. He assumed she'd roam those expansive rooms of her Fifth Avenue apartment for years to come, wiping her brow on fine wool throws and pouring a whiskey whenever she chose.

Then, just weeks after his conversation with Billy Jo, on a gusty early evening, he did see her. In a city of millions, in a constant commotion of people, he saw Corrine walking in front of him near the Morgan Library, her arm around a man whose arm also wrapped around her. She had never walked with Gigi like that. The man stood almost a foot taller than Corrine, his head bent toward her, rubbing against the top of her wayward hair. She wore a fur coat, and Gigi could see the ends of her scarves waving in the winter wind like happy flags at the ballpark.

Though he was on his way home and should have turned at the corner, he followed Corrine and the man as they walked north along Madison Avenue, heard her laugh at something her companion said. The man looked young, though dressed conservatively in a long topcoat. His head was bare, his hair light, almost blond. He leaned against her continually, talking, telling her things that made her laugh. Her laugh traveled on the air to Gigi, who walked behind her hunched in the cold. He didn't think about where they'd been or where they were going, only that they were so obviously together and that Corrine kept laughing and that the man knew how to make her laugh. With Gigi she had almost always remained aloof. To her friends like Billy Jo, she was dark and mysterious. She scoffed at Charles. Even his violence barely got her attention. She's a whore, Charles had said. You are one of many, he had said.

Gigi followed for blocks and then when he stayed behind at a red light, Corrine turned, purposefully. She found Gigi's face in the crowd, and she met his eyes and held on. The wind blew her hair madly in every direction and her companion kept her close to him, but she held her gaze on Gigi, a cutting, intense gaze. He couldn't imagine how she could have orchestrated such a random encounter. The light turned green, and a boxy woman in earmuffs pushed him out of the way. "Get moving," the woman said as she passed. "People got places to be."

He let the other pedestrians bump him along for at least another block, but his pace had slowed so that Corrine and the light-haired man got farther and farther ahead of him. Still, in the darkness and over the heads of all these strangers, he continued to hear her laugh. He thought it sounded light and happy, but that couldn't be true. She had just murdered her husband.

Finally he turned off Madison Avenue and walked home. He'd been to the drugstore earlier and now was surprised to find he still clutched the bag of toothpaste and aspirin. Once again Corrine had managed to lead him somewhere else entirely.

He hadn't thought the trial would intrude on the numb sameness of those winter days, but it did. The newspapers ran stories every day, often using a photo of Corrine looking lovely and righteous, a woman who knew what the camera could do for her. Bernice at the shop recognized the story. "This is the case that man came in to talk to you about." He'd nodded without looking up, hoping the conversation would end there. "Charles Bernard," she continued, reading from the *Post*. "His pretty little wife stabbed him a million times." She smiled when Gigi glanced up at her exaggeration. "Can you imagine how many wives in these five boroughs are rooting for this princess?" She chuckled and read the rest of the story to herself.

Billy Jo and her friend Jeannie decided that they needed to attend the trial whenever they could, as some sort of allegiance to Corrine. After the first week, Billy Jo called Gigi to tell him she didn't understand what good the New York State self-defense law was to anyone if these attorneys could still go after a battered wife like

Corrine. Hadn't she hit Charles in self-defense? Wouldn't he eventually have killed her? "It's so obvious," Billy Jo said, forgetting that Corrine had kept her marriage a secret from all her friends and acquaintances, that she'd spent stretches of time staying with Gigi in his apartment, and that she had, in the end, stabbed her husband without restraint.

But Gigi said none of this. He only listened.

"Here's the thing, Gigi. They're saying she didn't have to kill him. They had money. She could have left. There's no proof that he attacked her the morning she killed him. He didn't stab her first. She had no knife wounds or anything. And now with him dead all the money is hers. Maybe millions. Charles had these business friends who are all testifying that he was devoted to her, she was the light of his life, and she deceived him again and again, disappearing for days and weeks, wandering the streets like a vagabond, not even telling him where she was. All of that. It's all coming out. At least nobody knew about you," she added. "But she really looks like something. Ladylike and—that word Jeannie keeps using— demure. That's how she looks. Today she had on a white shirt with silver cuff links. So classy, honestly Gigi, you would hardly guess it was crazy old Corrine. Oh, I'm sorry. You probably don't want to hear all this. It's just so amazing to me that someone I know is on trial. For murdering her husband! The rest of us haven't even found husbands yet. She's only twenty-two years old—did you know that? Anyway," Billy Jo concluded, "it's something."

"I know," Gigi had to answer. "It is something."

The second week the prosecution finished its case and Lafayette Willson began his defense. Both the *Times* and the *Herald Tribune* appeared to favor the Park Avenue lawyer and his beautiful young client. Their stories referred to Corrine always as battered, beaten, or bruised. Frail and fragile. Thin. But the *Daily News* headline read "Child Bride Stabs Husband to Death," and the *World-Telegram* mourned the brutal loss of a prominent international businessman.

In Corrine's defense, Claire Bernard testified to the fact that her brother was often physically abusive to his wife, though she said he was remorseful and apologetic later. She said that part of his money was actually in a trust for Claire and some also for Corrine's mother in France. Corrine would not actually inherit all of it. Claire said that she'd known Corrine since the younger woman was a child, and always found her to be quiet and accommodating. Corrine would only have hurt Charles, his sister said, if she had to defend herself. Reading this account, Gigi remembered the way Charles had mindfully closed his sister's fingers around the handle of her pale blue leather purse after asking her to leave. And how she'd called out to him as the elevator door closed between them.

No other witness in the defense's case had specific information that Charles had abused Corrine. Lafayette Willson could call on no witnesses who had actually seen Charles hit her or had photos of her injuries. The doorman at their building could only say that Corrine had often been upset when leaving the building. He did agree that there were many days when she never came out of the apartment or never returned from some trip away from the apartment. Corrine's acting instructor testified that she'd seen bruises. So did a neighbor. But according to the prosecutor's cross-examination, all references to the abuse were hearsay.

Reading these accounts Gigi realized that he might be the only one who had ever seen Charles hit Corrine. Still it surprised him when she pounded on his door one night during the second week of her trial. She was not wearing the demure outfits that Billy Jo had been reporting, but the fur coat and scarves she'd worn the night he saw her walking on Madison Avenue.

"Are you going to ask me in?" she asked. "Or are you going to strand me out here in the hallway?"

He motioned for her to come in and watched, staggered, as she circled his table, her wide coat flaring. "Why did you tell Willson we were lovers?"

"Because it's true."

"So what, Gigi? If I'm in prison for the rest of my life what good is that gorgeous truth? You tell me?"

Struck by her anger, he stood on the other side of his table speechless.

"You know it was self-defense. You saw Charles punch me in the face. I had bruises every time you saw me. That's truth too, Gigi. You know it is, but you won't say. Why won't you say? Are you going to let me get convicted of murder because I didn't leave Charles for you?" Her voice continued to increase in volume with every question hurled his way. Gigi had no time to answer or even think of an answer. "You could save me. Claire tried to save me and you won't." She slammed her hand on the table. "Why won't you?"

"You could have left," he said finally. She paid no attention.

"You can still save me, Gigi."

They stood watching each other. She shook her curls and tugged at her scarves, but Gigi did not move at all. His body had locked him into such a rigid stance he barely knew he was breathing.

"You stabbed him eight times," he whispered.

"Well, you weren't there, were you? Maybe it took eight times."

"Why?" he asked, but his voice still faltered.

"Why what? Why get rid of Charles? Why use a kitchen knife? Why not run away with you to some thousands of lakes?" She was shouting by then. "There are no whys, Gigi. There's only you refusing to help me." She hit the table again and started for the door. In the hall she continued to bombast him. "You could save me and you won't. Oh my god, why won't you?" At that last question she sobbed and ran for the stairs. He heard her steps bounding down the two flights, then she slammed the outer door and was gone.

He sat at his table long after he turned off the lights, watching the uneven shadows crisscross his room. He couldn't do what she wanted, but her words made him doubt his resolve. Charles was horrible. He saw that in every arrogant word and sneer. Repair-man, he'd called Gigi. They hated each other, but she'd told him that is what they did. He had no part in that world, she'd said, that world on the sixth floor over there, where every pillow on every chair had been chosen for luxury. "We do what we do." He couldn't testify that she was innocent when he knew for a fact that she wasn't. Charles wasn't either, of course.

The next day Billy Jo called Gigi at noon to report that Corrine had looked lovelier than ever that day in a navy blue wool dress and matching shoes. She'd worn a blue felt hat that sat to the side with a ruffle of veil that partially covered her eyes. Billy Jo thought she might have been crying, poor thing. It was clear that she was not winning her case.

When Gigi and Billy Jo talked, neither of them knew what would happen next. Only at the end of the day did anyone realize that during the lunch break at the courthouse, Corrine had excused herself to go to the bathroom and not returned. She had not returned and she could not be found.

Someone gave the police Gigi's name. He suspected Lafayette Willson's team, since the police knew that he and Corrine had been lovers. But they also knew that Corrine had come to see him the night before she disappeared from the courthouse. They knew she'd been yelling in the hallway on her way out. She'd slammed the downstairs door. Neighbors had heard all of this and then when they saw the evening headlines, they had somehow put it all together.

He was at work when the two detectives came in and asked to speak to him in private. They asked questions about his relationship with Corrine and what he'd known about the abuse, about Corrine's general mental state, her mental state the night she visited him and yelled in the hallway. They went on and on, the two of them peppering him with questions, which came so fast that all he could do was blurt out responses, stammering and unsure of himself. He sat in the back room of the jewelry store for more than an hour with the two detectives nodding at his answers, as though the conversation were unfolding as they expected, while on the other side of the door he heard the muffled voices of his colleagues and Bernice laughing once and the bell over the outside door sounding again and again.

"Then you did see Charles Bernard physically attack his wife?" one detective asked, though Gigi had already answered that same question for the other detective.

Gigi nodded, looking back and forth between the two men, trying to read their position with him, what they really wanted. He didn't know where Corrine had gone, so he didn't understand why they kept at him.

"You didn't testify on her behalf."

"They didn't ask me."

"Why not? Nobody else witnessed the abuse."

"I didn't think she acted in self-defense. I told her lawyers that. I saw her crush a heavy doll onto her husband's head. Like it was nothing to her. I guess she thought I'd lie for her."

"But you didn't. I don't know, Paulo, she's quite a number. You sure you made the right call?" They both found this amusing. He could see that these men did not think he belonged in a league with Corrine and Charles Bernard. Which was his whole problem from the beginning.

The detectives went on to ask about Gigi's family, his possible Italian connections, whether or not he planned to travel anywhere soon. Even after an hour of his clumsy, honest answers, neither man appeared to believe anything he said. They ordered him to proceed as usual, to not leave the city until otherwise informed, and to let them know immediately if Corrine Bernard contacted him in any way.

After they left he remained on the metal folding chair in the back room for so long, Bernice finally came to retrieve him. "You're in it now, aren't you?" she said, more as a fact than a question. But she didn't press. Nobody at work pressed him. He finished up the day, took a taxi home, locked his door, and went to bed. He didn't eat or even have a glass of wine. In the morning he left early and walked into the north wind all the way to the shop. He kept his eyes on the concrete and moved when the crowd moved.

His name got mentioned in all the papers. The *Mirror* had managed to photograph him leaving his apartment, hat over his eyes, head bent down, coat collar up. Even to himself he looked like a shady character, like someone who might have helped a murderess escape so that he could meet her later on a remote island in the Pacific. "Jeweler Questioned in Heiress Disappearance" the headline above his photograph read. He appreciated that they had promoted him from a repairman to a jeweler.

Corrine's disappearance had ruined his life once again. He could almost think she'd done it on purpose, but he knew that wasn't true. When he went back over every moment and encounter with Corrine, he could only conclude that she had always had only one concern and that was herself. Funny that he'd never quite seen or guessed it. He thought she was a lovely lost young woman out on the streets of New York and he could save her. He thought surely he could save her. That's what she had screamed at him—that he could have saved her. She'd cultivated him so well, she believed he'd never let her down. And then he did.

Corrine's escape and Gigi's possible involvement did not stay news for long. It was just a week later when American Airlines Flight 1 crashed into Jamaica Bay after taking off from Idlewild, killing all ninety-five people who were aboard. The next day Wilt Chamberlain scored 100 points against the New York Knicks. Six infants died when a hospital nurse mistakenly put salt in their formula. The news kept coming, sensational and gripping. March and April passed with no sign of Corrine.

When the trees blossomed along Park Avenue, Billy Jo threw another party. Rites of Spring, she called it and hung pink and yellow streamers over her windows and doorways. Gigi went for her sake, smiled back whenever one of her friends smiled at him, but overall he preferred to hover safely near the nonworking fireplace on which Billy Jo had hung a little wreath of plastic flowers. Gigi was quite sure that almost everyone in the room knew of his connection to Corrine Bernard. They'd read the papers, heard their friends talking. Maybe some of these people had been Corrine's friends too, though Corrine did not have many friends. Only a hardy soul like Billy Jo would have bothered with her.

A few days after Billy Jo's party, and almost three months after Corrine left the courthouse to never return, a teenage boy popped into the jewelry store, his eyes darting from one corner to the next until he spotted Gigi. The boy waved nervously. "You Gigi?" he asked, and when Gigi nodded, the boy handed him an envelope and ran out the door with the urgency of someone who had just robbed the diamond case. Bernice was with a customer, and the part-time girl had taken her coffee break, so only Gigi witnessed this curious moment.

He turned the small, plain envelope in his hand. His name was not on it. Nothing at all had been written on the envelope, but it had been held or touched or passed along enough to show wear—a smudge, a slightly dirty fingerprint, a bend at the corner. Maybe the boy who delivered it had caused the distress or maybe it had traveled a distance to reach Gigi there in the middle of the morning in the middle of the jewelry store. He took his sharpest knife and slit the top crease. Inside he found one piece of heavy paper, a type of cardboard torn from a larger sheet or a lightweight box, a scrap really. Gigi pulled it out and read the words written in black ink in the large unmistakable letters and loops of Corrine's hand: *Do not find me.*

For a second he lost his eyesight, heard nothing, gripped the scrap of paper, and leaned forward on his desk. She always got him. She always did. Gigi sat holding her note until he saw that Bernice was walking her customer to the door. He quickly put the paper into the envelope and both into the pocket of his coat. He took up the pliers he'd been using on the repair in front of him, but his hands shook.

"That woman is a gold mine," Bernice beamed as she crossed the room. "Every time she walks in the door she ends up spending a thousand dollars. I just made enough to take you out to dinner after work Friday night, Giovanni. Calamari at Elio's?" Then she noticed the tremors in his hands. "Are you all right? Gigi? You're as white as your shirt." She hustled into the back room and brought him a thermos cup of coffee. "I put lots of sugar in there. Get your blood going again."

Gigi avoided her eyes, but he drank the sugary coffee, and holding the hot plastic cup, steadied his hands. "Thank you," he said looking down at his work. "Something just came over me."

"You need a girl, Gigi." Bernice took back her empty coffee cup and greeted a new customer coming through the door.

Hours later when her husband picked her up after work, Bernice insisted that they drop Gigi off at his apartment. Once alone and inside he took out the envelope and removed the note again, feeling as though he were dealing with a message from the dead. *Do not find me.* This note was no different from her intense stare at him near the Morgan Library in the winter. I dare you, that's what she meant. I dare you to find me.

Gigi spent all night thinking about where she might be and how she managed to get that note to him. Ever since she disappeared from the courthouse in late February, he'd supposed that she'd left town, that the light-haired man in the overcoat or someone like him had pulled up in an expensive car and hurried her over the state line, maybe to Canada, maybe to a tiny unknown village along the coast of the Atlantic or even farther. Back to France. He never thought she'd be close enough to get an envelope delivered to him. Every time he began to believe he might move past his obsession with Corrine, she came back to him.

The next morning he wrapped up his pretty purple violet and walked to his sister's studio apartment. "I can't take care of this anymore," he said. "You need something cheery in here." He cleared a spot on the small table by her bed. "Just water it once a week and keep it by this window."

She panicked. "I don't understand plants, Gigi. What are you thinking of? I'll kill it, you know I will."

"I might be leaving soon, Bella. Whenever the cops say I can go."

"Oh no. It's this whole Corrine business. Please stay. I know girls who would love to meet you. Singers like me, all those single clerks at the store. I even know an Italian girl who makes panettone for Christmas. Mia. She's so pretty. Don't give up on New York, Gigi. Don't go." She started to cry.

"I can't leave the city until they say I can, so don't worry yet. Just look out for the violet."

"What are you going to do without it on your red table? That's where it belongs."

"I don't think it does, Bella. Maybe I'll just put a bowl of fruit there, like Ma used to do. A bowl of oranges maybe."

The police had also told him to let them know if Corrine contacted him in any way. But he told no one about the handwritten note on the scrap of paper. He told no one that she'd returned in dreams looking as she had before he'd actually met her. She came back now wearing only her scarves, her body delicate and smooth. She never spoke. Nor did she shake her curls. Nor did she avoid his eyes. These nights Corrine walked through his dreams barely breathing, waiting, wanting something that not even Gigi in his fitful sleeps could give.

Seven more months went by before he got permission to leave New York. It took him only another month to give his notice at work and pack and plan his trip. He gave his red table to the newlyweds across the hall, and on an unusually warm February morning in 1963, he boarded a train that took him to Chicago and Minneapolis and, finally, home. He sat by the window in the train car and watched every daylight hour move by, every smoky depot and frozen lake, hundreds of scattered farms and small towns where school buses waited for the train to rumble through, and pale skies and crystal blue skies and the sun that fell out of view, vivid until the last.

THREE

November 16, 2011

The phone woke me up at seven this morning, jolting me out of a deep night's sleep in my mother's chair. "This has gone on long enough, Meg," my husband's voice barked at me. "When the hell are you going to get back? You've already missed three of Tony's games. Mick won't do his homework. I'm sick of Subway sandwiches." He is reminding me that I am not a free agent at will to stare into the tall, narrow pines and contemplate my father's life. I have my own life. My husband is tired of Subway. "We have no clean towels here, Meg. None."

"I know," I assured him. "I know."

"It's almost two weeks. Two weeks!" Just hearing his own words inflamed him all the more.

"Well, my dad died." He hung up when I said that. Being a businessman, my husband knows when a meeting is over.

It might be that I have never understood marriage. My mother died so soon, that I can hardly remember how my parents were with one another. I mostly remember how they were with me. I remember my mother teaching me mindless household tasks, chatting away about her friends and her friends' kids or what she planned to cook for the holidays, fixing her hair, touching up her lipstick, always in a shirtdress and half apron. And, of course, I remember a lifetime with my father. But I learned so little about how a marriage might work. I saw Aunt Natty and Bill muddling along as they did, being kind and useful together, not saying much. Uncle Bill actually said almost nothing. I have never since known a man of so few words as Uncle Bill, who exercised an entire repertoire of communications without them. He'd nod and chuckle, shake his head fast and slow—depending on the context—he'd smile or half smile or slap his knee, lean forward or back, a veritable human dictionary of nonverbal responses. But I never caught the exact gist of their marriage.

I had an idea that my father's sister Mary and her husband made a marriage worth the trouble. They'd escaped to California together, after all, so they only had each other for a while. They must have been a team, those two. But because they lived so far away, I never really saw how their bond worked, or how running away to a new state might have melded them together. I would have liked to know that. It might have helped me.

And I never met anyone who wanted to bound across the country with me to a life all our own. I might have, if I hadn't married my husband when I did. But I think at that time, almost twenty years ago, I didn't consider the largeness of marriage, how another person could shape your days into something lovely or not, how a husband could bring in a whole set of positions about living and put them on you, insist you encounter them every day—routines and expectations, friends you don't like and activities you're not asked to join and needs and more needs and jibes and jokes you don't understand. I had not thought about any of that, because my father had been so easy to live with and had loved me so well. How could I have imagined?

But I have options, of course. We all do. I have resources, friends, opinions of my own about living and my own routines, I suppose, my own quiet jibes here and there. And when my father called me, I left everything to play out the end of his life the way he wanted it played.

When I was twelve, maybe thirteen, we got an invitation to visit my father's second cousin Santina and her husband, Tom, who lived in a tiny town in Michigan called Iron River, with only a few streets and a narrow trickle of brown water moving through. Our happy relatives took us in and fed us plates of homemade macaroni with meaty sauce and pitchers of lemonade. Unlike Natty and Bill, these two talked constantly, interrupting each other in good cheer and asking questions without even waiting for the answers. They had one son then living in Milwaukee, and they said they missed him every day. We couldn't even sleep in his room while we visited them because, "he left everything just the way he wants it," Santina said without apology. My father slept in the spare bedroom upstairs and I slept on a daybed out on the screened porch, an adventure of squeaky springs and a view of the night sky.

On our second day, Santina took me to the local general store and bought me my first pocketbook. That was her name for it. The bag had a handle and a snap closure and was made of pale pink patent leather. I could barely speak, I felt so elevated. Before we left, Santina gave me a handkerchief printed with large daisies and Tom gave me a five-dollar bill to put in the zippered pocket of my new bag. "Ciao bambino, ciao Giovanni. Come again, come again," they called as we pulled away from the curb to drive home. But we didn't go again, and I cannot say why. My father liked them, though, I could tell. That Christmas, he refurbished a beautiful old Bulova watch and sent it to Santina in thanks for our visit.

"They're happy," I commented to my father, making conversation as we hit the highway for home.

He glanced over at me and smiled. "Santina met Tom the week she stepped off the boat, Meggie, and they've been crazy about each other ever since."

"Really? Like love at first sight?" I remember how much I wanted the details of their story, how juicy it seemed to me then.

"It happens," he went on. "Sometimes a person can get taken away by another person in a minute. Maybe less than a minute. It's just there. Like you found what you've always been looking for. And you never want to let it go."

"Is that what happened to you with Mom?"

He didn't answer, but took his eyes off the road just long enough to meet my own. "Your mother was the sweetest person I ever knew. She was kind and she was easy for me."

At that time I was too young to understand the enormous value in "easy." At that time, riding in the car with my father, I wanted a more dreamy, heart-stopping story than he was willing to give me. I pumped him further, certainly, but he said no more about falling in love. Not then or ever.

When I brought my future husband home, what did my father see? We did not act madly in love. We were never a giddy or sweetly affectionate pair. We were not fierce or passionate either, not the type to scream and throw pots, then make up intensely for hours, like Elizabeth Taylor and Richard Burton. I think my husband and I were always basically functional. We did what couples were supposed to do—bought a house together, had two children, went to dinner and movies, did tasks, bought gifts now and then, made love on a regular schedule. We signed up for marriage, and that's what we did. Not necessarily tenderly or wildly or even hilariously. And I don't think either of us ever really fell in love.

One of the women I taught with years ago told me over lunch that if her husband died before she did, she'd just as soon throw herself into the grave with him. "I couldn't live without him," she'd said, setting her lunch-meat sandwich back on its plastic wrap and shaking her head. "I couldn't go on."

My father did go on without my mother. I never knew him to show an interest in any other woman, though I saw that women always liked him. The year after my mother died, I would often go to my friend Janice's house after school to do homework or play games until my father could pick me up after work. Just before he came to the door, I'd notice Janice's mother dabbing on her lipstick and taking off her apron. She'd meet my father at the door, she'd call him by his first name, and ask if he'd like a fast drink before going home. He always declined, but he did so graciously, as was my father's way. Women appreciate graciousness. Besides his graciousness, my father remained handsome and well groomed. He held himself tall and maintained eye contact when he listened. The women he encountered responded to that, just as Janice's mother did. "You have such a nice dad, Meg," she'd say. "Poor man."

He lived alone for the rest of his life. By myself in his space, I think I understand how he managed all those years after I left. He had his routines, his things collected over decades, the clean air and, in these later years, the clean lake and its scores of eager fish. I am not hurrying to finish here. I like the feel of late fall, the fading energy and muted colors.

I am sitting on the porch step drinking yet another cup of coffee when a red Chevy truck lumbers down the drive. An older man with a shock of dark hair jumps from the truck and strides toward me like he knows me well. "Margaret," he booms, stretching out a worker's hand. "Jimmy Vusich." He pumps my arm heartily, his face needing a shave, one front tooth missing, his eyes bright as the afternoon sky. "I finally meet Gigi's Margaret."

His reference to my name surprises me. "My dad called me that—Margaret?"

"Well he did, I believe he did." He grins. I take him in, trying to remember if my father ever mentioned this friend. "Nobody like your dad," he says. "Cripes I'll miss him." He sits on the step next to me, a man comfortable with himself, and takes in a deep and heavy breath.

"You fished together?" I want to give him a spot, a place in my father's life.

"Some, we fished some. But your dad was his own man with fishing." He chuckles. "No, me and your dad used to sit in the cabin here and just, you know, just gab. Your dad and me, we could solve the world's sorrows and more. Enough gin, we could even solve our own."

"You want to come in for some coffee?"

"Well, I might do that. Your old man made some cup of coffee, you know that? Strong as hell. Cripes, Giovanni, I'd say, you brew coffee like an old Finlander—make your hair stand on end. It's Italian espresso, he'd say. Espresso! Where'd he get that idea?" Jimmy guffaws as he circles one of my mother's chairs. "Mind if I sit here?" he asks, then settles in before I have a chance to respond.

"Are you a widower too?" I hand him a mug of coffee and sit in the opposite chair.

"You might call it that." He grins again, the gap showing in his teeth. "My wife left me years ago for Vegas. The good life." He raises his eyebrows. "Somewhere in there she died, and we never divorced, so I suppose that makes me a widower. Mostly I've been on my own. Do what I want. Smoke if I want." He smiles and takes a swallow of his coffee. "I asked your dad once why he never remarried, good-looking guy like him. He says, 'Jimmy, when I catch my limit, I get off the lake.' So that's it."

People don't die when they die. For years they might tell you things you never knew, leave pieces behind you never thought you'd find. The life they led breathes on. Six months after my mother died, my father found half a dozen jars of pickled beets in the cellar hidden behind her applesauce. Now why would she have hidden these, my father asked me. But neither of us knew. She could hardly have been trying to surprise us with pickled beets. I never even liked beets. And now after his own death, my father has already left me a mysterious note, chose not to remarry because he'd fished his limit, and sat for hours with a big, old friend named Jimmy who is missing a front tooth.

"My dad didn't want a funeral," I say. "He made me promise."

"Oh sure. We all have our ideas, Margaret."

"I don't even know what was wrong with him. He called so late. He wouldn't go to the hospital or try to save his own life. My husband says I killed him. I could have called, I could have pushed. But—now it's over." Jimmy listens carefully, letting me tell my side of the story. "I don't even know what happened. My husband doesn't like that either. 'What the hell happened up there,' he says." I am relieved to say these things.

"Nothing you could do," Jimmy offers. "I'd stop by a couple of times a week. Sit here. Listen to the crows squawk. Nothing you can do."

"But he didn't say? He didn't tell you?"

"What's to tell? You get sick, you get sicker. We talked about the lousy economy. The Twins. Local news. The weather." He watches me closely. "Cripes, who wants a bunch of doctors meddling? He liked it right here. Guys like me and your dad, Margaret, we don't care much for meddling. I don't even get this tooth fixed. Who cares?" He smiles extra wide. "You don't care, do you?"

"No." I smile back. "You know I found a note in my dad's hand-kerchief drawer yesterday. It says 'Do not find me.' Do you know anything about that?"

Jimmy repositions himself on my mother's chair. "We all have our secrets, I guess."

"Did he ever talk to you about New York? He lived there before I was born. My mother always thought something sad happened to him there, but he never said. He'd never go back. I wanted him to take me, but he'd never go back."

Jimmy Vusich's eyes do not leave my face, but he shows no expression, gives me no window. Then he says, "A loose end, Margaret, that's all. He had a good life. Whatever happened back then didn't keep him from catching those fish, fixing my old watch here. That's what you got to think about now. The life he had. You and your kids." Jimmy's voice cracks and he looks away until he can recover himself. "Anyway that's it. If you ever need any help out here, just give me a holler."

"I was thinking it might be too much to keep the place."

"I see that. Cripes, you've been packing like a squirrel out here. But it's good property, Margaret. It's good property." He nods to emphasize this truth.

"I know."

"You can always unpack a box," he says. He is a kind man and my father was his good friend. Before he goes I give him my father's Woolrich plaid jacket, which he puts on immediately, patting the pockets with satisfaction. "Smells like your old man," he grins. He wears the jacket as he walks back out to his truck. He jumps in like a man much younger, then turns to yell, "You can always unpack a box, Margaret."

For an hour after Jimmy leaves I roam my father's property that is now my property. I kick through the dead leaves that have accumulated along the shore and stare out across the quiet sheen of Lost Lake. By the time I return to the cabin the sky is darkening. I look around the house, at the glow of my father's few lamps in various corners of these three rooms and at the boxes I've packed, cardboard intruders that they are. I can't even remember why I have been so eager to abandon this place forever, why I launched into the cleanup with such lonely fervor. I guess that's what people do. They divest and move on. Who wants all that past chunking along behind you when you are full-speed ahead on some sleek forward highway?

When my father first planned to move out here, I asked him how he could bear to leave the house in town after all those years. "I grew up here, Dad," I chided. "It's my home." He was packing up these same kitchen utensils then, the eggbeater neither of us used very much, the dented pots with their ill-fitting lids. For several long minutes he acted like he hadn't heard me while I stood alongside him, hands on my hips, a young woman with a legitimate gripe I thought. "I want my children to know this house, to sleep in my old room and sit on the porch like we used to do. I want them to make hot chocolate on the same stove where my mother made it for me."

At this my father stood up to face me. "I want to live in the woods," he said. "That's my choice now." I didn't argue anymore. I helped him move, as was his choice, and I continued to live in Minneapolis, as was my choice.

"You choose," my boys used to say when we'd eat out and the unwieldy plastic menu seemed too large and confusing. "You choose, Mom."

This idea of choosing exhausts me. It means I have to take bold action. First I have to weigh and think and decide. Then I have to take action. No wonder packing these boxes has seemed less difficult than making a careful, calculated choice. Now I suppose I can unpack the boxes, as Jimmy Vusich said. I can spend another several days undoing what I just did. If I choose. "You choose, Mom."

"Why did you go to New York?" I once asked my father, and he said, "Well, Bella was there and she wanted me to come. Pop had just died. I was up for an adventure, I guess." So did my father actually choose to go to New York? Did he think about the possibilities and consequences of leaving this northern town for New York? Was it a meander or a march? And even more complicated is the question of his return here. Was that a choice or another accident of circumstance?

Outside is a glorious night and I am part of it in this cabin tucked amidst the skinny pines. I wander into the bedroom where my mother's painting hangs guard over the bed with its pale chenille coverlet. The note I found sits on top of my father's dresser where I left it last night. I pick it up again and turn it in my hands, as if it will tell me something more. Something to make all clear and ease my sadness. I cannot honestly imagine that anyone would not want my father to find her. I cannot imagine what he could have done to provoke such a declaration. The letters are printed boldly, digging into the paper. Fast, hard strokes of pen onto a thick, half-torn scrap of paper. Why would my father have wanted to hang on to a note like this through all these years, through his marriage and my childhood, his retreat to Lost Lake and decades fishing these cold waters?

I put the note in its worn envelope and back into the drawer. Then I unpack the box where I've stacked his handkerchiefs. I arrange the drawer the way I remember, place the boat key next to the Timex watch and the fishing licenses. I check the Gruen on my wrist, which, of course, maintains its perfectly calibrated measure of time. I have restored some order, my father's order and my own.

In the living room the phone is again ringing. "Mom!" Tony shouts in my ear. "Dad says you have to come home. We have mice now. He says it's too much." He lowers his voice. "It's a mess around here, Mom. Plus I have things to talk to you about. Like things."

When my sons plop down at the kitchen table, they might ramble on for an hour or more about this class or that, some jerk in math, a fight in the cafeteria, the coach's new haircut. They cover ground, and this kind of happy wandering doesn't happen on the phone. I tell him I miss talking to him too. "But I need a few more days before I'll be home," I tell him.

"She needs a few more days," I hear Tony yell to everyone within a block of where he stands. And then my husband is on the line.

"What on earth now, Meg? This is starting to be some kind of *Twilight Zone* episode. Gigi died. Of what? You take weeks to do— what? It has to end. We're a family here. How on earth do you expect me to work full time and keep up with the kids and feed everyone and have clean underwear for god's sake? And now we have these damn mice on the kitchen counter eating our leftovers. It's out of hand. I don't give a damn what you're doing up there. I want you home tomorrow, Meg. That's it." He pauses to let his message sink in. This time I hang up.

And the instant I hang up, I know that my husband has crossed a line, the kind of line kids draw in the dirt with the toes of their shoes. Cross this line and I'll eat you up. Cross this line and I win the game. Or you lose the game. All these years in my cordial, cool marriage the line has been there between us, taunting one of us to cross. Break your mother's back. Capture the mountain. Now he's crossed it and I think there will be no going back. I sit in my mother's chair in my father's cabin in our part of the world, where bears amble through without notice and deer and owls keep watch and millions of fish multiply in thousands of lakes. My husband is on the far side of the landscape, maybe back where the thickest of trees temper the light. His face will grow more vague each day and the farther he recedes, I know, the less I will even notice.

FOUR

September 22, 2011

Yesterday I rowed out to the center of the lake, listened to the pull of the oars through the water. I sat for two hours memorizing the colors of birch and oak against all these pines out here and kept my line in to see what might happen in perfect weather in midafternoon. Sure enough, those little crappies surfaced and toyed with the minnows, let themselves be caught, one by one by one. But I threw them back, as I have for weeks now. I have no appetite, let alone for tiny fish out of my own Lost Lake.

The eyes are always wide. These are not creatures that look the other way and ignore the fact of death coming. I've been grateful to them for all the years I've fished, since I was a boy in my father's boat. They always came to me easily, even when others fishing on the same lake sat livid and frustrated from one hour to the next. But look at those people, I'd think, even when I was in high school and surveying my grown peers on the docks and shores. They've got their sacks of sandwiches, packs of cigarettes, some even have radios, not to mention coolers of beer, out for a lark, these men. What fish would want to swim toward all that? Even to grab a squirmy, tasty minnow or a whole fat earthworm?

My father had the technique, but he could not match my deep connection with fish. I've never told my secret, though I tried to demonstrate it to Meggie back when. She was the wrong age, I think. Or she has the wrong disposition. Maybe that's the problem for everyone but me—they have the wrong disposition. I take nothing with me onto the lake. Not the work waiting for me later or the conversation I might have just had or the news headlines screaming in all directions. Not the weather. Not what might be causing that old dog to bark like crazy on the other shore. I take nothing. I stay under the surface of the lake, under the ice in winter. I stay low and silent and content, as though I too am swimming in deep waters looking instinctively for my food. That is my secret. They say the best cops are the ones who can think like criminals. That's how it is. I am like the fish and, as a result, they come to me. They always have. But now I don't keep them. I let them eat the minnow and splash back into the lake.

I'm dying, of course. I don't need a doctor to tell me what these sharp pains and lack of appetite mean. I don't need to sit on a plastic chair at the clinic to wait for a complete stranger to poke me and take tests and tell me, gravely and politely, what I already know to be true. All the years I repaired jewelry, I never thought about what had caused a clasp to break or beads to fall off the chain. I took the problem for what it was and moved forward from there. Now I'm sick, and the whole world would tell me to do the same thing with my body as I did with thousands of necklaces over the years—move ahead and fix the problem. Except I know I am unfixable. Or that the fixing will take something from me that I don't want to lose. No fix will let me stand at the edge of my own parcel of land and look out at the moon as it quarters and slivers in the sky or the tiny crappie as it grabs my minnow and goes.

I do not believe that any fix would leave room for Billie and Betty and Ella. The fix will be all about the fix. Chemicals and stents and tests. Maybe surgery. The fix will turn me inside out, and I will not live anyway. If I thought I could be fixed, I'd try. But that isn't the case. I'm no fortune-teller, of course. And God has never spoken in clear language to me, not ever. Yet I know. Let's say I have gone into still waters with this. I'm dying.

The big problem is my daughter. I have never wanted to trouble her. No girl who loses her mother when she's only ten years old needs to be troubled any further. So thinking it over these past weeks, since my body first railed so violently against me, I have decided to let the leaves turn their shades of gold and red and fall as they do and to let the air change as it will and to keep this ravaging illness to myself until there is nothing she can do to feel responsible. Until close to the end, when I will want to see her pretty face one more time.

My daughter has such a pretty face, a sweet, round, symmetrical face. Unguarded, really. Open. Looking back, I'll say I made a mistake not teaching my daughter to be more on the lookout. Oh, I'd tell her about the deep lakes, the thin ice, the worry of hungry animals. I taught her to recognize poison ivy and to keep her eyes on the road when she drove a car. But I did not teach her wariness. I did not teach her to raise a flag into the wind and pick up its direction. It's so easy to be fooled. I was fooled as a young man, because my parents never thought to warn me about the many dangers that might await me once I left our well-ordered household. I think they never thought to warn my sisters either. Francesca who went to war with high expectations and died within months, Mary who bounded off to California hardly to be heard from again. Nat who hunkered down, but died young anyway and Isabella who, like me, encountered the unexpected in New York City. None of us left home prepared. Then I was too lax or overwhelmed or full of hope for my daughter to prepare her either.

And so she married a man who does not seem to know how to love her. I saw it right away. I saw it, how little he looked at her. Men in love with pretty girls cannot take their eyes off them. You know what I am talking about. They hang on to every blink of the pretty eyelashes, every small gesture that pulls the hair back or swats the fly away or picks up a blueberry to pop into her mouth. A man in love seizes all this like his own dear prize, then glances around to see who else might be noticing his amazing good fortune at having won such a girl.

But not my son-in-law, Robert. We always call him Robert. He is never Rob or Bob or, God forbid, Burt or Bobby. My son-in-law is named Robert—period. Not only did I see that Robert chose not to watch my daughter as young men in love do, I saw that he had many people around him at all times, buddies and brothers, cousins in every direction, nephews, uncles, men around him all of the time. I saw that he remained busy. Robert is a busy man. He goes to work, where I am certain he is never not busy, and after work he runs and bikes, swims and talks on the phone, he takes care of his property, as he likes to call it, and dashes off for supplies and returns and throws ball with his boys and hikes on vacations. The thing is, love can never be that busy. Love has to sink down in a chair sometimes and watch the gray sky not move.

I remember summer evenings as a boy, when my parents sat side by side on their red metal lawn chairs and said nothing and did nothing until just before dark, when my mother would stand up, smooth her dress and head for the house, holding the door open for my father until he followed her, always with some comment to her about letting in the mosquitoes or moths. That is my idea about love—serene and intimate. My daughter does not have that.

I didn't have it much either. When I married, I was still recovering from my own foolishness in New York. My wife was easy and kind, relieved not to be alone any longer. She tended to me and to our home and then to Meggie. She relaxed with me at night, which I always so appreciated. But I didn't have enough time to love her the way I believe love can unfold. I hadn't been infatuated at the start, as I think a man should be, loving even the way his girl kicks off her shoe and how it might hang there balanced on one toe before it clumps gently to the floor. Like I said about young men in love. I didn't have that feeling for my wife. But I loved the person she was and the mother she became.

I loved her buttermilk pancakes and her little doilies on the furniture, so old-fashioned and pointless. I loved that. I loved her pink mouth every day at every hour, no matter if she was mopping the floor or heading out the door to a PTA meeting. My wife loved her pink lipstick. If she hadn't died so young, the two of us eventually would have come to the kind of love my parents had. I believe that.

After she died, I focused on Meggie. After Meggie left, I turned to Billie and Betty and Ella again. I let those women sing to me and lull me and remind me and take me wherever I wanted, just there on the phonograph. Have you ever listened to Betty Carter sing "Tell Him I Said Hello"? The long slow syllables, the wanting, the piano's trill, the brushed drum, the clarity. *Just tell him I said hello.* Hello going so far into the basement, you think you will not hear it again. And then it returns. *Hello.* Or what about Ella Fitzgerald singing "Too Darn Hot," hitting every word with a punch, punch, punch. *I'd like to coo with my baby tonight, pitch the woo with my baby tonight.* I could go on and on.

But Billie Holiday has always been my number one. My sister Bella says it's because I feel sorry for her, her crummy life, raped and prostituted before she was fifteen, jailed, abused, abandoned. It was a miracle she lived to see forty, let alone made hit records and millions of dollars and changed the way a blues song rolled out for the rest of time. Billie Holiday knew so much blues in her life, she breathed and bled it. Listen to her sing "For All We Know." Her voice quivers, she hesitates before each word, waiting for it to come to her, through her, as if she's singing this for the first time and only to you. The odd lilt comes and goes, so at the end, when she sings *Tomorrow may never come*, the *may* tips upward, moves you over her way, before she ends *for all we know.*

I own every album Billie Holiday ever made, including her out of print *Velvet Mood*, which I bought in New York in 1960. She'd died the year before, so I didn't imagine I'd ever find a copy, and then there it was, the cover corners torn, the record pristine. I still play it. I still play them all, along with Frank, Perry, Nat, Johnny Hartman, Lena Horne, Rosemary, Mel—all my crooners. I haven't replaced any of the LPs with discs either, a fact of enormous hilarity to my grandsons, who never even met an LP until they discovered mine.

I don't know if Meggie will want the records, and I'd like to be able to sort all this myself, not leave it for her to ponder. I'd like to pack it up the way I did when I moved from town, but I don't have the energy. Yesterday I spent an hour in the boathouse just studying my tools, picking up one and then another to feel their weight and cool metals, what we've done together, me and my tools. "Grampa can fix anything," little Mickey said one visit. He's right. From clogged drains to flickering lamps, warped doors and leaky boats, I'm your man. And those are my tools. Maybe Meggie can keep them for Mick and Tony. You never know what will interest a boy. Certainly my mother didn't think I'd be listening to "colored ladies" all my life. But here I am. *They can't take that away from me.*

My wife and sister Nat died suddenly. My mother died within days of a stroke. My father doddered about in sorrow for a few years after he lost her, not really sick, but sad and uninterested in whether he breathed or did not. So I have no real experience of knowing death is coming, feeling it dig away as I do. Sometimes when I look in the mirror to shave, I see the man I've always been. I am so clearly alive, that I cannot believe I am dying. How can I soon not be? It's preposterous.

An older friend of mine who lived in town used to come out and fish with me, the second-best fisherman in Saint Louis County, in my opinion. Last winter I didn't hear from him—these old guys aren't much for the telephone—so I stopped by his house one day when I went in for groceries. He didn't look too bad, wrapped in an afghan his wife had crocheted years before in shades of yellow to orange to rust, graduated color that matched the furniture. "Hey, Joey, how you doing?" I asked him. All guys up here have cheerful, boy names like that. Joey, Jimmy, Paddy, Eddie, and so on. This is not a culture that supports men who want to be called Lewis or Vincent. Or Robert. That is a fact.

When I greeted Joey, he pointed to a fifth of brandy and nodded for me to pour. Then he said, "Gigi, you're never ready to die. Look at me, ninety-seven years old. I've buried my best friends, my wife, all my brothers. You'd think I'd be ready. Of all people, you'd think I'd be ready." He drank his brandy and I stayed quiet. "Life is a flower," he said then. "It's here and in a minute, it's gone." He looked me straight in the eye to stress his point, a man who'd fought in World War II and worked in the mines and lived a man's life in the north, but who understood that his life had lasted not much longer than a flower's. He smiled, acknowledging the truth of his own statement. "You'll see," he said.

That was early March. He died in June, and I went to his funeral along with the few dozen others who had outlived him. We sang the old religious songs those priests love to hear, and Joey's remains got blessed and buried, and his grown children piled sprays of spring flowers on top of his grave.

Now I see Joey every day. I hear him every day. And wherever he is, I will be there soon, if there is a place, an actual place. I like thinking there is, though I cannot imagine what sort of place could hold the souls of millions and millions who have died since the beginning of life. Of course, the universe is beyond imagination. Why should death be less so? And why should there not be a place? Why should I not see my mother and father again or my wife or my sister Francesca, whom I barely remember, or poor Natty, who died holding on to her vacuum cleaner?

After President Kennedy was killed, the magazines ran a photo of him walking a beach along the Atlantic, his pants rolled, his feet bare, the powerful ocean wind mussing his perfect hair, and Kennedy looking out to sea. That was their image of dying, I'd say, and not a bad one at that. I try to call it to mind these days, think of myself in that way, barefoot and staring out to sea, the wind whipping me about, the universe pulling me into its vast roar and significance.

I prefer this image of the vast universe to medical science right now. I prefer to concentrate on a certain romance about living and dying, like my old friend Joey telling me life is a flower. "You'll see," he'd said. And I do. I ease my pain with stories of my own life, stories only I know and that will die when I die. Tell me this is an exercise in lonely futility, and I will tell you that meaning is not everything. When I fixed a watch, I realized there would be a point when it would wear down again, that Dr. Riley's wife would bring back her husband's timepiece again and again, and I'd fix it and for a while all would work well. Until it didn't. Is there meaning to that? I make a meal and eat it, and it's gone. The earth turns and turns and turns. I think there is little meaning. Only truth.

So I am traveling back over my own truth. I do this without effort, the stories march on from one hour to the next, and then return from the other direction, like a band of soldiers on drill or the high school drum and bugle boys, my stories march on tirelessly. I'd like to tell you that my truth is uplifting, that I've loved the life I've lived. Mostly, mostly. But there are parts of my truth that don't settle, never have, that nag at me. But I can't avoid these any more than the charmed ones. They come anyway. They're tireless, as I said.

When I was a young man, I knew a girl who killed her husband and ran away. But that's too simple a version. After my father died I took a train to New York City to be near my sister Bella. I saw a girl and got so immediately taken that I could not shake her from my mind. I was 23, and I fell in love with a figment. But who thinks that at the time?

I'll tell you what I did think at the time. I imagined her an orphan, of sorts, a poor girl out on the streets. The first time I saw her, she was sitting in a small bar eating lunch, relishing every crumb, focused on her food the way I remember being at the end of the longest days wandering out around DuPont Lake. Hungry. She looked so hungry to me—and beautiful and wayward. I expected the girls in New York to be smooth and pulled together, sophisticated. Then the first girl I really noticed was not any of that. Her hair hung loose and curly, her coat seemed too big, she wore all these scarves and ate like she hadn't eaten in a day, at least. So I made my assumption that she was in need.

In fact she was married to a rich French businessman with an enormous apartment just north of the Metropolitan Museum on Fifth Avenue. She wanted to be an actress doing tragic roles like Joan of Arc. Heroic, dying women. She never actually told me that, but I knew. One day she demonstrated her skills for my sister by trudging desperately across my floor pretending to be a woman in the desert. Bella loved it, clapped at the performance and, at the time, I remember feeling pleased that they had taken to one another. Still it seemed an oddly painful performance overall. I didn't know she was married at that time. I didn't know her husband hit her, punched and pinched her, tightened his hands around her throat. And I certainly didn't know that she'd run away from him to me or that soon she would kill him.

So that's what I was up against, young Giovanni Paulo from the flat land of Northern Minnesota. I fell in love with a girl I thought I would rescue and maybe marry and sit with in the evenings listening to Billie Holiday sing "Jeepers Creepers." Instead I watched her smash her husband's head with a garish, heavy ornament and then toss that hair of hers, like she'd just tidied up the room and needed a moment's rest. She didn't kill him then with me as a witness. He rose up again that day, I suppose, though I did not stay to see it happen. I left in a daze and stumbled home. It was summer then. Summer in New York, and her husband didn't die, and I had just learned she even had a husband.

Her name was Corrine Bernard, and several months later she stabbed her husband to death with a kitchen knife. The police arrested her for murder, but her attorneys wanted to prove that she killed him in self-defense and wanted me to be the one who told her wretched tale in court. But I'd seen her fight back with more ferocity than a tribal warrior. She shocked me beyond my experience when she walked over to her husband that summer afternoon in their grand apartment and slammed him in the head with a gold-trimmed figurine. I watched him twitch and collapse. And then she offered me a whiskey. So when her attorney asked me to say she'd killed her husband in self-defense, I didn't do it.

All my life I've wondered if I made a mistake. Her husband had surely been a brute, a frightening and righteous man. Maybe he would have killed her eventually, so maybe she was acting in self-defense when she stabbed him eight times in the middle of the morning. But I didn't say that at the time and, as a result, it looked like she would go to prison.

So, of course, she ran away. She walked out of the courthouse building at the lunch break in the second week of her trial in February 1962, and disappeared. For months the police tried to find her and couldn't. Then in June, a boy, nearly hysterical, ran into the jewelry store where I worked and handed me a note. She hadn't signed it, but I knew it was from Corrine, her sprawling handwriting, the dramatic loops and the large letters. You almost lost track of what you were reading, you'd get so distracted by those flagrant lifts and dives. That was Corrine. Her note said: *Do not find me.*

The note was a taunt. She pulled me in and mocked me at the same time. But I didn't find her or even try to find her. I kept the note, I have it still, but I never told anyone and, just then, in the summer of 1962, I did not find her. I waited for the police to tell me I could leave New York, because they had their idea that I might be an accomplice, and when they told me I could leave, I came back home. I got a job at the best jewelry store in town, married my wife, and bought a house with a front porch on a block just a half a mile from where I grew up. Then came Meggie. Then came my wife's death, then Meggie's graduation, her marriage, her two sons. Right about the time Mick and Tony came along, I sold the house with the porch and moved out here to Lost Lake. You see how the stories of my life march along, all in step, each falling in line, always in the same place, never altering.

When I packed up the house in town, I kicked up so much dust the past billowed in clouds around me. I found my father's fishing hat, an unraveling straw number with a faded black band around it. I found a stack of greeting cards I'd given to my wife over the years we were together, drugstore cards with the occasional glittery decoration that disintegrated all over me. She'd tied them with a bit of pink ribbon and tucked them so far in the back of a drawer, I'd never stumbled across them before. I found the bright yellow school patrol belt that Meggie was probably meant to turn in at the end of fifth grade.

It took me twice as long to leave that house as I thought it would. I kept making discoveries and each discovery took me back to a place I'd forgotten, and each of those journeys became its own sweet moment. I enjoyed myself immensely then. I believed I had many more stories ahead of me. A cabin on a lake waiting. Two baby grandsons. I could wander back though time, knowing I was still moving forward. What a luxury that seems to me now.

In that sorting, I found Corrine Bernard's note. I'd kept it all these years in its smudged envelope along with the postcards of New York that I'd bought when I lived there, glorious shots of Central Park in spring, arty black-and-white photos of the Flatiron Building, the Empire State Building, the New York Public Library, a ferry boat out on the harbor. Standard New York views. And one plain envelope from Corrine Bernard. I pulled it out from the postcards and carried it in my shirt pocket the rest of the time that I was packing up the house and unpacking again out here. I moved it from one flannel shirt to the next as that week went on. And finally, when all got settled here, I put the envelope into the top drawer of my tall bedroom dresser next to my fishing licenses. It's still there.

At first I had too much to do to really consider her message again. I had all my tools to hang and organize in the boathouse. And I wanted a boat. I shopped for the right motor. The cabin required some attention, paint and repairs. Everyone knows what it is to move into new space. You have work to do. You have to wiggle around some to find your best fit. Then it was one thing after another. The ice froze over and I had to get out to the fish. Meggie came with the babies. I made a few new friends out here. Pretty soon, several years had gone by.

But every time I opened that top drawer to get out the boat key or one of my handkerchiefs, I'd see the note. I never forgot Corrine anyway. All my life. Her image, her delicate hands and beautiful face came to me almost every day, like a tune I could not shake, a phrase that continued to repeat no matter where I was or what I did. I thought of Corrine on my wedding day and on Meggie's wedding day. She would float through, flicker, leave, return. Her taunt to not find her, though, did not stay with me always. Maybe I just blocked it out as an afterthought in our short, awkward relationship and not what my mind clung to. No, my mind hung on to my early impressions of a wayward girl that I might save, a girl who came to me in dreams before I'd ever heard her voice. A girl I made up really. A figment, as I said before.

I remember the day I decided. I'd been out on my boat coaxing a walleye along, a sizable walleye that followed, but wasn't quite ready to grab on. And just when I thought he would, the sky rumbled and began to darken quickly. I pulled in my line and puttered back to shore, but I didn't quite beat the torrent, which hit me and my boat hard. A fierce spring rain stings when it strikes, so soaking wet and fumbling to get out of the fray, I trudged into the cabin and immediately lit a fire in my stove. Then I turned on my radio to hear what kind of storm I was dealing with this May afternoon. "Don't find yourself outside," the announcer said. What an odd phrase, an odd command I thought then and mulled it over as he rambled on about the southerly direction of the storm, its origin in Canada, the velocity of the wind.

I sat by my fire, drinking what was left of my morning's coffee and listening to the pelting of the rain on my roof. Corrine appeared then, as she had throughout those almost forty years, and I began to count it out. She'd be around sixty, about four years younger than I was at that time. I might not even recognize her, as happens when memory locks a person at an age long gone. I concentrated on her until the rain had stopped and my fire had burned low. I sat as the evening slipped into night, fading in and out of the present, remembering and considering. And I decided to find her. It didn't seem impossible. I might be able to locate Claire Bernard in New York or some Bernard families in Paris. I had financial resources and time. My decision to find Corrine happened that simply, in a late afternoon storm. *Do not find me* she had written in 1962. Then in the spring of 2000, I set out to do just that.

It took me only days to get quite close to where she might be. I looked through phone books at the public library in town and tracked down an address for Claire, who appeared to live in the same apartment where she had lived back when, on East Eighty-Seventh Street. Just finding her address awakened New York for me again, its pulsing industry and fine details, the men in their tailored suits and hats, the women wearing fitted dresses with shoes that matched, the way Claire Bernard did when she'd breeze through the jewelry store door with her expensive childhood pieces. Her gold locket with Corrine's photo. I thought about rainy days in New York when the sidewalks were all umbrellas, mostly dark and dignified, the occasional silly dime-store contraption turned inside out in the wind. I wondered if the Upper East Side maids still walked babies wearing perfect pastel knits and if the cabs still blasted their horns at every truck, pedestrian, and fellow cab. I thought I'd like to see the block where I lived, walk Madison Avenue at dusk, look for my old places—the jewelry store, the corner grocery, the little French restaurant where Corrine ordered crème caramel and painstakingly licked her spoon.

I made my plans without telling anyone but my neighbors to the north, a couple around my age who have lived out here since they got married in midlife and appear to have no family and almost no connections to the rest of the world. They have always liked me, I believe. I keep up my property, I am the reported best fisherman around, and I don't drop by their cabin unexpectedly. These are all tenets of a great neighbor when you live in the woods.

I bought my ticket, flying nonstop into Kennedy airport, which used to be named Idlewild when John Kennedy was still president and didn't need to be memorialized. I bought my ticket, then I did something nobody in my life would ever imagine I'd do—I booked a room at the Stanhope hotel, across the street from the Metropolitan Museum. I can't tell you how many times I walked past the Stanhope the years I lived in New York, how I'd watch dapper types going in and out, the bellman opening car and cab doors, always thinking, young Gigi Paulo, of what it must be like to stay in a hotel right across from the grand art museum with its flags flapping in the wind day and night and the ghosts of ancient art resting so near.

I allowed myself ten days, a travel extravagance beyond anything I had ever done. I have never been a wanderer. I am a man who lives in a cabin on a lake with little I want beyond what I have.

But Corrine Bernard always caused me to move outside myself. How I tromped the streets of the city looking for her so many times and laid awake all night just to watch her body roll toward me and away in the streaks of moonlight that came through my large, barred windows. I think of following her sister-in-law to their apartment and insinuating myself and stumbling down Fifth Avenue later, always in a state when it came to Corrine. So how could I be surprised that, at age sixty-four, I had booked a room at the Stanhope hotel to go and find this woman who had explicitly written for me not to.

On Thursday the first day of June, my neighbors gave me a ride to Duluth, where I got on a plane to Minneapolis, then on to New York. I had never seen New York from above and the day was bright, so there it all was, the rivers around, the park its own unmistakable patch of green, buildings clustered tightly. I confess I cried. I'd left years ago on a train chugging through gray tunnels and, there I was, returning like a bird, soaring over the East River, a middle-aged man who had managed to live pretty well all those years in between.

The cab ride to the Stanhope cost more than my yearly fishing license, a fact I deliberated as I counted out my bills. But this trip had nothing to do with frugality or common sense. In this trip I had become like the country squire of *Don Quixote,* who leaves his ordered life, dons his armor, and sets out on his impossible, but goodly quest. No one who worked at the Stanhope recognized me as the young man with all his dreams. They greeted me respectfully, assuming my membership in their club of successful patrons, and, to be honest, I felt I was part of that club. Though I'd never stayed in any hotel other than a Hyatt in downtown Minneapolis, my soul took comfortably to the small, polished elevator and the heavy flowered drapes. The bathroom gleamed in creamy white tiles, and I remember thinking that if I built a manor of my own, I would surely create bathrooms just like that. I mean to say, this tasteful sort of luxury did not jar me, as you might think it would. I hung my clothes in the closet with a true sense of proprietorship, like a man at home.

Claire Bernard lived in a building without a doorman, but with a bell and intercom system. The voice on the other end said, "Miss Bernard's residence. May I help you?" I explained that I was an old friend in town after many years and gave my name. After several minutes, the door buzzed, the voice told me to come to number 814, and I went into the building. At number 814, I knocked and was greeted by a woman about my own age with gray, cropped hair. She wore wire-rimmed reading glasses on the tip of her nose. "Miss Bernard says she remembers you," the woman said, not bothering to introduce herself. "She doesn't get visitors, really, so it's a surprise." Then she smiled, but only a bit and walked ahead of me with her head thrust forward, her glasses still perched on her nose. "Let me know if you need anything," she said as she led me into a large bedroom, nodded, and went back the way we had come.

Claire Bernard's apartment had grand high ceilings, windows over Eighty-Seventh Street, and floors carpeted from end to end. The walls of the rooms I walked through had been painted pale colors, blue like the summer sky, gray like a November fog, pale yellow, and beige. The large bedroom where I stood was blue with several portraits on the walls, all of grave, but attractive people against deep black backgrounds, framed ornately in gold. The furniture fabrics matched her walls and so did Claire, dressed in a sky blue robe and sitting in a wheelchair near her bed, her body caved in on itself, the hands and feet gnarled.

"Hello." She tipped her head to the side to meet my eyes. "Are you looking for Corrine again?"

Her condition had set me back and her direct question even more so. "You have a lovely home, Claire. I'm glad to see you," I said.

"How did you know?"

"Where you lived? You are in the Manhattan phone book." I had walked closer to her and drawn a chair near so that I could see her face and hold her gaze.

"No, not where I live. How did you know she's returned? How would you know that?" She sounded very upset with me, as though we'd been wrangling about this for days, as though half our lives had not passed in the interim. "I don't know what to do about you and Corrine."

"You mean she's been gone all these years?"

Claire raised her eyebrows. "What else?" she answered. She was not the same woman I remembered, polite and comely. This elderly Claire Bernard, crumpled into a wheelchair, showed her anger, her mistrust, and impatience. She was gray and sick and alone.

"I didn't know," I said. "But I did come to see if you could help me find her."

"Why?"

"You're the only person I thought might have kept a connection."

She shook her head. "But why find her?"

"I don't know, Claire. Because she told me not to."

At that, Claire laughed a light, gay sort of laugh, exactly like she'd laughed on her quick visits to the jewelry store. The lines around her eyes crinkled in humor for a minute—so I laughed too.

Then she rang a bell that sat on the bedside table and asked the woman with the reading glasses to bring us some tea. "So I'll tell you," she said. "When Corrine left in 1962, she went to Montreal and then to Saint John's in Newfoundland and over to Denmark, of all places. She had aliases, I presume. She never saw her mother again, because she thought it too risky, but it broke Mireille's heart. Such a dear, my friend Mireille. For the rest of her life she apologized to me for her daughter killing my brother." Claire rolled her eyes. "Charles. He was always such a bully." She kept looking at me as she talked, even when the woman came in with a tea table on wheels and set it in front of us with gold-rimmed blue plates that also matched the room and a basket of pastries with butter and jam. "He was always a bully. Except to me, because I was two years older and my father adored me. There's always a long story, isn't there, Giovanni? My father found Charles an enormous disappointment—a short, squatty child with no obvious ability. He couldn't play soccer or sing or make good conversation. He wasn't popular at school. He cheated on tests and got caught. He hit some girl who told all. So it went. But then all that bullying seemed to work for him in business. Or whatever he did. He knew how to get ahead, certainly. He knew how to make money. Anyway, Corrine's mother died a few years ago. She used to write me every week, all those years. Do you like this tea? There's a new store on Madison Avenue that just sells tea. My assistant—her name is Judy—she rolls me over there now and then."

"It's very good, Claire. At home I sometimes drink peppermint tea."

"And where exactly is home?"

"I live on a lake in Northern Minnesota. It's quite civilized."

"Oh, I'm sure. You look exceedingly civilized to me. You live alone?"

"Yes."

"I see."

"Is the jewelry store still there?"

"No. Gone." She smiled just the way she used to. This is how it can be as we get older. A gesture comes through from the person we once were, some wayward bit escapes from whoever we used to be.

"Did Corrine stay in touch with you all those years?" I asked.

"In a way. She had this friend, very bold and completely devoted to her, who was willing to go back and forth for her, deliver messages, pick up money—because I continued to support her with Charles's money. Well, it was her money too. But it all went to me after he died and she fled. So this friend of hers kept us in communication. He took his chances. That first year I thought the police watched me constantly. But her fellow would show up like some kind of spy, sidling up behind me in a crowd or pushing next to me at the museum. Can you imagine?"

"Do you know his name? Who he was?"

"Never. I can tell you every pair of expensive shoes I ever saw on his feet. I knew the sound of his voice the second I heard it, but he didn't have a name or a place or a number where I could reach him."

"Did he let you know Corrine was coming back?"

"I haven't heard from him in a couple of years. She had plenty of money, I suppose. And I don't know what he was to her. Did she marry him? Who runs errands like that for so many years?" She shook her head and looked to me for an answer.

"We are lots of fools," I answered.

"I have seen that. I wouldn't have known." From her awkward position, she kept her eyes on me.

"Did you ever marry, Claire?"

She laughed that laugh from before. "I had two opportunities," she said. "I let them both pass."

"But why?" I wanted to think that a nice person like Claire Bernard would have encountered luck and someone to love her.

"My mother ran away before I knew her. My brother's wife killed him and she ran away too. All things considered, living alone looked predictable and comfortable to me. When I was young, some men liked me very much. Even you, Giovanni, might have liked me if you had not been so taken with Corrine. I lived in attractive good health for most of my life. I think it was enough. I sometimes wanted more, craved it even. But I always had enough. At the end of the day, I've enjoyed a pleasant meal and good lighting. This tea. Such lovely tea."

"Has Corrine's return changed anything for you?"

She had to work at drinking her tea. The angles her body had bent into did not allow her to easily reach for a cup or hold it, tip it, or drink from it. Still I saw that she had figured all this out for herself. It just took time and concentration. "Corrine changes nothing," she said at last. "She came by once and the sight of me folded like a street vendor pretzel was clearly enough. She calls. She has some place in the East Village. Another grand adventure."

"Do you know why she came back? After all this time? It's hard to understand."

"Well, who is talking, Giovanni? She came back to see what might still be here, I suppose. Nobody's hunting her anymore. Corrine came back to make some more trouble for herself, that's what I think. It's what she knows how to do. Her poor dear mother. I cannot tell you how different Corrine is from her mother." Claire studied her arthritic hands. "There was a time when I thought she was such a charming girl. I was glad to bring her here with me when she finished school. I had hopes."

"What happened to change her?" I asked and waited while she considered my question.

"Nothing," she answered at last, looking up from her hands in that crooked tilt that I was getting used to. "Nothing happened. I turned out to be wrong. That's all." She looked back at her hands.

I stayed for a short time longer and promised her I'd call her before I left the city for home. She gave me Corrine's address and made me take a small tin of the tea with me. "Such a lovely tea," she said again, and I thanked her.

From Claire's, I took the subway to the East Village, got off at the Bleeker Street station and wandered. I bought a pack of cigarettes, so that I would not look conspicuous out on the street. I had smoked possibly a half-dozen cigarettes in my entire life, most of them when I was hanging out at the Sportsman's Café in high school. But I unwrapped the cellophane and lit one immediately.

According to the address Claire had given me, Corrine lived in an old brick building on East Second Street just off the Bowery. I walked that block for several hours holding one smoldering Marlboro after another, hoping she'd come home or leave or even lean out one of the windows. When my precise Gruen told me it was seven P.M., I left. It was a Thursday evening in June. At home the whole town would be quiet except for a few bars and the ballparks. But in New York, life rocked along at full pitch, as it always had and as I'm sure it always will.

I hailed a cab, but I didn't go directly to the hotel. I asked the driver to let me off at a restaurant called Elio's on Second Avenue, where my coworkers from the jewelry store used to go for calamari whenever anything good happened or anything bad or anything that they thought required calamari. I think I hoped to see them there, maybe all in their seventies and eighties, but still wearing their pearl chokers and bright lipsticks, still thin and bossy, waving at me from a table in the bar. Instead I ate alone. I ordered the calamari in their honor and toasted them in silence. I gave the calamari a fair try, but honestly, I'd prefer walleye any day. Nonetheless I soaked up the sauce with bread and chatted with my waiter and walked back to the hotel in the fading evening light.

I was not successful in seeing Corrine the next day, Friday, but when I arrived on her street early Saturday morning, armed with a new pack of Marlboros and coffee in a take-out cup, there she was, talking to another woman on the sidewalk outside her building. Just as I approached, the other woman laughed and crossed the street, and Corrine glanced my way. I won't say she recognized me instantly, but almost. Almost instantly. She had changed so little, her hair still a tangled mass of curls and still the same color. She had remained fragile looking, waiflike as I had thought the first time I'd seen her.

I walked up to her and said as calmly as I could, "Hi, Corrine. It's Gigi."

She didn't move. She didn't smile or speak. She stood struck and silent until her eyes squinted at me and she hissed, "Get away from me or I'll scream right here on the street. Get!"

This response startled me so much that, for a minute, I actually could not go away. I couldn't get the message to my feet to turn and go. But she didn't stop her tirade, spitting out threats that I couldn't translate into either meaning or action. "I came to see you," I remember saying somewhere in there, begging I suppose, all the dignity of my age and experience faltering before her. "I came to New York to see you." I'm sure I said that at least twice in the midst of her commands for me to leave, to go, to get out of her sight, how dare I and so on. Then when I finally started walking away from her, she yelled, "Gigi," and I spun around to face her. "Where are you staying in New York?"

I told her and she nodded. Then she let herself in to the old building where she lived.

She left me so rattled, I walked those Lower Manhattan neighborhoods all morning. It's a blur to me now, because with every step, I considered the woman I'd just seen and the beauty she'd maintained and her cruel edge too. I thought about what Claire had said—that Corrine had returned to New York to create more trouble, that trouble was what she knew. As I walked across Chinatown and Soho, up and down streets I didn't bother to note, I evaluated myself. I am a cautious man who never ventures out on thin ice. I wait for the layers to form. I test the thickness. I do not tend, as the radio announcer had said during the spring downpour, to find myself out in the storm. Yet there I was, in Corrine's circle of trouble again and wanting more.

She came to me that night. I had hoped she would and actually thought she would, because it was her bent to take charge, to chase me away from seeing her only to come around and see me on her own terms. The desk clerk called to say she was in the lobby, and I went down for her. She had dressed for the Stanhope, in a small black dress, patent leather shoes, and a tidy purse that she held close to her body like a book. She wore a stunning Baume & Mercier watch, heavy and detailed, enormous on her thin wrist.

"That's a wonderful watch," I said before saying anything else.

"I know. I bought it today. There's a vintage store on Wooster." She ran a finger over the curves of the watch as she spoke. "I paid a fortune for it too. These old watches are not cheap, you know."

"They're worth it," I said, comfortable with this topic, thinking it was serving us well so far. I kept talking about old watches as I escorted her to my room upstairs. Once inside with the door locked behind us, she took off her shoes and sat in the one soft chair.

"You look good," she said to me. "Not bald or fat. Good haircut. Nice shirt."

"You look good, too, Corrine. The years cannot have been too terrible for you on the run."

"I would have preferred to stay in New York, Gigi. I would have preferred you to come to my defense, so I could have stayed and acted and maybe made my mark, instead of hiding in one backwater place after another. Just to be clear."

"Anyway you do not look like a woman who has suffered too much. You look beautiful."

"Beauty comes from suffering," she said, and I could tell she was performing for me, reciting lines she'd arranged for herself. "When you suffer, your eyes become larger, they expand to hold the tears, the muscles in your face give in to it, you pull yourself higher, trying to rise above your pain, and after many years, voilà, you are more beautiful than before."

I didn't respond. I thought that if my daughter heard such a speech she would laugh hysterically. Who talks like that? And maybe this quick connection to my daughter showed on my face, because Corrine said, "Are you listening to me, Gigi? You're impossible. I wore these horrid little shoes and came all the way up here to your hotel, and you're glancing out the window. There's nothing out there," she said. Then she smiled, which also seemed part of the performance.

"I'm sorry," I said. "I have a daughter who always wanted me to bring her to New York and show her where I lived, but I wouldn't. I never came back until now."

She arched her eyebrows. "And now you miraculously find the woman of your dreams again. Aren't you the lucky man?"

I sat down on the edge of the bed close to her chair. She'd painted her toenails a dark, deep red and wiggled her toes freely as she sat. "Corrine, I don't know why I wanted to see you again. The note you had delivered to the jewelry store that said not to find you, I kept it. I live out in the woods on a lake now, and I have lots of time to think and wonder, I suppose. I just decided to find you and came here, and it's all been so easy. Here you are like before. Just like before. Maybe that's all I need. Just to see that you're good, that you're alive and good."

"You didn't come to apologize?"

I drew back. "You killed him, Corrine."

"He was ridiculous. Horrible and ridiculous. I haven't regretted it for a day."

"I know he wasn't a nice man."

"Nice?" She snorted. "He was horrible."

"You could have left. You could have married me. It's what I wanted. I wanted to protect you and take care of you."

"In the Minnesota woods? Are you joking, Gigi? One look at me and you had to know that wouldn't work."

I didn't answer. She was right, but that is no argument against the intensity and determination of a young man's love. Or the fantasy of what could be. Even then, in the Stanhope hotel room, I had to fight not to reach out and hold her feet, massage her toes with their dark red nails. I had shown little reason ever when it came to Corrine.

"I'm dying anyway," she threw out.

"You are just saying that."

"No. I came back to die."

"Of what, for God's sake? You look like the picture of health." I could hardly stand how good she looked.

"These things lurk, Gigi. You live on a lake. You should know things lurk."

"Tell me what lurks, Corrine."

"I don't think I will. But it's true. And now you've found me and you can remember me this way, in a nice dress at this nice hotel having our little chat about old times. Do you want to chat anymore about the old times, Gigi? What happened to your pretty violet?"

"I gave it to my sister and it died," I answered.

"Of course. Singers and actresses can't take care of pretty little plants. They can barely take care of themselves." She smiled knowingly. "And Bella? She's well?"

"She just moved from New York to Manzanillo, Mexico. She has a husband. She likes the air there, she says."

"Does she know you're here?"

"Nobody knows. Not even my daughter," I said, not sure at that moment that I should have left without telling Meggie.

"Tell me about your daughter then. What is her name?"

"Margaret. I call her Meggie."

Corrine's eyes flashed. "Ah, Margaret. I knew a Margaret in school. Marguerite, actually, in French. She was exceptionally tall, so I remember her still. It's good to have something people remember, isn't it, some peculiarity all your own? You, Gigi, have those blue eyes. If I wanted to remember you well all these years, I would think about your blue eyes. But many times I would only think how you didn't save me, how my life might have been if I'd stayed in New York and become an actress. I can't help but wonder." Then she added, "There is a poem about a child named Margaret. Have you ever heard of it? I remember it from school." When I shook my head, she said, "I'll find it for you. That will be my parting gift, Gigi. A poem for your daughter before I die."

"You aren't dying, Corrine. It's theater. It's your own play, like a one-woman show."

"Gigi, you know so much! You are an amazement, everything you know. Yes, yes, this is my one-woman show." She threw her arms out to take in the imaginary stage lights. "And where is your wife?"

"She died young." I didn't want to talk about my family with Corrine, I realized. They were like Lost Lake to me, a pure and private place that had nothing to do with the turmoil I created for myself in New York. "Did you marry that young man with all the blond hair? The one walking with you on the street the night I saw you? On Madison Avenue?"

"God, Gigi, you remember everything, don't you? Do you remember my cashmere scarves, too? Or maybe you didn't know they were fine wool, my scarves."

She was taunting me again. I knew that. I opened the small bar and took out two bottles of wine. "Do you want white or red?" I asked.

"So civilized, Gigi. So debonair. But the man with all the blond hair loved me more than you did. He had just graduated from one of those pompous New York private schools and claimed his inheritance and put himself at my disposal. Forever. He did what I wanted, went where I wanted, bought what I wanted. In return, I kept him as happy as I could. Anyway he was hit by a truck outside Paris two years ago and died in a minute. But he was never my husband. I had enough of a husband at a very young age." She shrugged slightly.

We drank the wine, Corrine in the chair and me on the edge of the bed and just then, I believed the relationship between us to be as significant as anything else I had known. "I wonder if that bistro down by my old apartment is still there," I said. "Where you ate like you were starving. You always ate like you were starving," I added.

"The bistro is still there. I walked by it. And I often am starving, actually. Who do you think cooks for me, Gigi? You think Charles did or my blond companion? Only my mother and you ever fed me." She poked my leg with her painted toes. "Do you still make meatballs?"

I nodded.

"What else?"

"Anything. I fry fish from the lake, I make soup, eggs. Meat and bread. I eat well out there in the woods."

She laughed like I'd said something very funny. "Of course you do," she said. "Take me to our bistro tomorrow night. Then you can come see where I live. I'll get a nice Italian wine for us. Some Barolo, top-notch." She laughed some more. "What do you say? I'll make you happy that you found me."

My voice caught in my throat. "Do you want to stay tonight?" I asked, hesitant, hopeless.

"Of course not," she answered and picked up her shoes to put back on her feet. "I'm fine. I'll go home. Meet me at the bistro at seven tomorrow night. Don't be late," she said, and she left. I watched her walk to the elevator, immediately lost within herself, and certainly lost to me.

"Good night," I called from the door of my room, but she didn't turn or answer. The elevator came, and she stepped in.

I didn't sleep well that night, unnerved by things she'd said. That I'd ruined her chances, that she remembered my eyes, that she was dying. I had no way to sort what was true from what was not. Usually Corrine spoke some truth. Her mother had been French. Her husband had been cruel. She had suffered. Finally I focused on my grandsons' faces and Meggie and the afternoon horizon on Lost Lake. Then I slept, long and deep, until I heard a knock on my door late the next morning, announcing that housekeeping was there to clean my room.

At six P.M. I headed for the bistro. It was busy and I had to wait for a table. I waited twenty minutes to be seated, then another twenty minutes for Corrine and another. Still she did not come. I drank a glass of wine and ate a basket of bread. I tried to look as though this was all part of a plan, this waiting for someone who did not arrive. I studied the menu assiduously, silently trying to translate the names of the French foods. Coq au vin, for example, is rooster in red wine. But maybe you already know that. Finally I put down three ten-dollar bills for everyone's trouble and left at almost nine.

It took yet another twenty minutes to get a cab, so that by the time I pulled up in front of Corrine's brick building that June night, the sun had set. Her building had no outside light, but the door was not locked. Inside I heard voices upstairs and moved toward them. At the second-floor landing the doors had been propped open to a high, cavernous space where two men sat smoking and arguing over a sculptural structure in the middle of the room. "Excuse me," I said, and they stopped in midsentence to look at me in their doorway. "Do you know where I can find Corrine Bernard in this building? Which apartment?"

The darker and more handsome of the two men asked the other a question in a foreign language I thought might be Middle Eastern and went back and forth with him in this way until he answered, "There is a woman on the first floor, but we don't know her name. Maybe she is your Corrine."

"I didn't see any doors downstairs," I said.

The second man nodded vigorously. "Behind the stair," he said, motioning to the back of the building. "Behind." His handsome companion nodded in assertion, and they both smiled encouraging smiles. The sculpture between them was of nothing I could recognize, but it loomed like a living thing, reaching tentacles of metal out into the room and toward me. Dust and residue covered the floor and the men's faces too, and their tools lay all around them, odd and purposeful implements also covered in dust.

"It's good," I said, because I wanted to say something to those men, who like me, worked with their hands and their tools and made something of it all. "Whatever it is." They laughed and nodded again, and waved like we'd all been friends for a very long time.

Downstairs I followed the hall to the back and found a wide door to an apartment directly under the one where I had just been. I knocked carefully and called out to Corrine, but even after several tries at this, I got no answer. Then I turned the doorknob, found the door unlocked, and took a step inside to see if I might find her. I entered a similarly expansive space to the one upstairs with painted wood floors and narrow, but tall windows at the front and back. A grouping of chairs surrounded a low table to the front and several mattresses stood stacked one on top of the other at the back of the room. The only light came from the street lamps outside, so I had to scan the room in shadows. One swatch of light wavered across the assembly of chairs, but I could not make out where Corrine might be in the room.

I called to her again, almost in a whisper, and kept squinting in the dark for what, I didn't know. I had the idea in my head that some emergency had caused her to miss dinner at the bistro, a sudden illness, a recurrence of whatever she thought might be lurking, as she had said, ready to do her in. I disliked the whole situation—her missing dinner and me hovering about furtively in this apartment that might or might not even be hers. "Corrine?" I called again quietly.

I heard nothing but the cars a block away on the Bowery. But as my eyes adjusted to the dim light, I saw that there might be a person in the pile of blankets and quilts covering the stacked mattresses at the far end of the room. I inched forward, not wanting to intrude, yet needing to know. At that moment I mostly wanted to be with the men upstairs, who were arguing about where to go next with their sculptural reaches, the metal curves and plaster trim. I should have given them the Marlboros in my pocket or gone out and brought back wine. I wanted to hear their stories and learn what landed them in that worn space creating such work. Instead I continued to shuffle toward the bed, where I could now see that Corrine slept under layers of covers, with only a knot of curls showing. I got close enough, then, to hear her breathing.

I sat down on the floor near the bed. Outside, traffic maintained a constant hum, and the street lamps gave that shaft of light in the front of the apartment. At some point I thought to shut the door and lock it, but otherwise we spent the night this way, Corrine and I. I don't remember what I thought, if I thought anything. In a sense, I had my line in, waiting for what might surface. I remained alert and ready and watched the light reaching halfway toward me across the floor and listened to Corrine's quiet breathing.

When the sun rose, I saw the rest of the apartment, a white stove against the long wall next to a wall-mounted sink, the old kind like my parents had in the house where I grew up. Some tenant, surely not Corrine, had attached a green flowery skirt to the sink, just as my mother had done, a device to hide what might be stored underneath. But nobody had hung curtains on the windows or laid rugs or put pictures on the walls. I did not see any obvious sign of the Barolo wine Corrine had said she would buy for us. With the early light, I stood and stretched and paced the length of the apartment. I thought I should leave. I didn't know Corrine anymore, if I ever had, and whatever her life had become, it might not be any of my business. But I didn't leave and around seven that morning, Corrine sat up in her bed. She focused on me immediately.

"What are you doing here?" she said, clearly not happy to see me standing in the middle of her barren apartment.

"We had a date at the bistro," I answered.

"Does this look like a bistro to you? It does not look like a bistro to me. To me, it looks like where I live, by myself, and pay my rent and expect my privacy."

"The door wasn't locked," I said. "I was worried."

"You are always fucking worried, Gigi. Where does it get us?" She was sitting rigidly in her bed holding the covers against her chest and confronting me once again.

"It's okay, Corrine. I'll go."

"You never face the complexities, do you? Even now, you're almost an old man and what do you see? Your longtime sweetheart. The girl you left behind. All rosy. All dreamy. And if there is a problem, you worry. But here is the thing, Gigi, I didn't plan to have no father or to marry an asshole. I didn't plan any of it or to roam around without purpose all my life and never really make my mark. I'm a ghost, Gigi, a fucking ghost. And you're part of that. All your worries and honesty or whatever you say, you cast me out to wander like one of those lepers in the Bible. And now you come back to see if I'm fine or good or whatever you think I am. I'm not, Gigi. I'm not."

"Why did you come to visit me at the hotel?" I asked, still standing in the middle of the room, still trying to think my way around her rage, find logic, fix the problem. "I mean you seemed glad to visit."

"Did I? I have my relapses. I have my curiosity. I have nice dresses I want to wear." Saying this, she started crying, loud and furious crying. "Go, Gigi. Shut the door." She had to say it again before I moved, and when I was just about to leave, she told me I should not return.

You see the pattern, how this woman always pulled me in and pushed me back or lured me close then leapt away. Just before I unlocked the door to let myself out, I turned around. "Listen, Corrine, I was not the trouble then, and I am not the trouble now. You've always toyed with me like I was nothing, like I never mattered at all. But I tried to matter and do right by you and I still am trying to do right by you, sitting on your floor all night waiting for you to wake up and see the light of day. I didn't murder Charles, you did. We could have had a nice dinner last night. I thought we could. Why not? Maybe I'm a dreamer, Corrine, but you—you know how to ruin anything." I surprised myself with this speech, a flurry of words so unlike my reserved self, but I didn't surprise her. Corrine had made her way in God knew how many unknown cities and towns from New York almost to the Arctic and back again, and she'd taken a knife in rage and thrust it in and out of her husband's body eight times. Nothing surprised her.

When she didn't respond to what I'd said, I left. I started walking back uptown and when I had no more strength around Madison Square Park, I flagged a cab to the hotel, where I slept for hours. If I dreamed, I didn't know it. If anyone came to my door, I didn't hear. I was the athlete who trained and tried and hoped to win, but did not. And the defeat had worn me to my core. I had no plan when I decided to find Corrine. I had not considered any particular outcome, only the finding. My task was to find her, see her, place her in the world again. I didn't think about what we would say or do. So no matter what happened I wouldn't have been prepared.

I had almost a whole week left in New York. I went to one museum after another, ate lunch in their cafés, watched locals talk intensely across small tables and families of tourists straggle in looking tired and confused. I bought toys for Mick and Tony in the gift shops. One day I wandered Central Park from early morning until the music started up at night. I ate from the vendors, strolled through the zoo. Each evening I returned to the Stanhope, where they greeted me with familiarity and asked me how my day had been. On my last night I went back to Elio's. The waiter remembered me and joked with me like we were old friends. I'll say, in this way the neighborhood places in New York are pretty much like they are at home. Once people take note of you, they remember you as one of their own. I ate spaghetti and meatballs, not quite as good as mine, but satisfying nonetheless.

All week I hoped for a message from Corrine, and at least once a day, I'd feel tempted to go back to where she lived and try one more time to connect with her. I'd imagine that she was ill, and

I would need to get her to a hospital. I would see myself calling Claire with updates and sitting by Corrine as she recovered. In these concoctions, I'd extend my stay in New York, do whatever it took to save her this time. Or I'd imagine going back to her apartment and finding her dressed and puttering around her place with its whitewashed floors, chipped and uneven. We'd go to the bistro or to some hole-in-the-wall in Chinatown, where every bite of food tells an old country tale. We'd hold hands. She'd say that, yes, she had loved me in some way. That is the sort of foolishness I entertained, which got me through my evenings and my long wanderings and in and out of museums all over town.

But I did not hear from Corrine, and I did not return to her apartment. My last image has her sitting across the room from me in her bed piled high with coverlets and telling me not to come back.

Still I'm not sorry I returned to New York. When I was young, I believed I owned something of the place, even though I lived only on the edge of the buzzing energy. But I felt it to be my own, New York. The color and hustle and grit, the corner groceries and small restaurants and handsome strangers and constant skyline. I could have dreamed it all in my most perfect dreams. So I came home to Lost Lake full of the city and tried not to think about Corrine. Two years later I got a call from Claire Bernard's assistant, Judy, telling me Claire had died. Her lungs had collapsed. Judy said it was a blessing, like people so often say. Not existing is apparently better than deep suffering, though I can tell you that I do not look ahead to my own death as a blessing. But then I haven't suffered horribly. Unlike Claire, I have not been caved into a wheelchair for years looking up at the world in sideways glances, struggling to breathe, feeling pain every day.

With Claire gone, I had no more access to Corrine. I assumed she moved on from her dilapidated apartment off the Bowery. I assumed she lived, and still lives, in spite of the death she said was lurking within her. She is the largest story of my life that has no resolution. I tell it over and over to myself, as if the next version will end in a different way. I will be there or she will be here, the sun will set gracefully behind us. But always I end with the upset of her anger and the Barolo she never bought and most likely never even meant to buy.

The crows have screeched madly today. I wonder what agitates them, for when I scan the birch trees, I see only late summer light between the angular branches. I do not see any cause for their restlessness and complaining—no owl or fox or bear ambling by. Their dangers, like my own, remain unseen. But crows have the instincts to sense trouble in their midst and to squawk like crazy to one another in alarm. One crow lifts awkwardly to a higher branch and looking up to follow its movement, I catch the light on my face, full on my face, dazzling and warm.

FIVE

November 19, 2011

My husband has not called me again, though the boys continue to report. It will be Thanksgiving next week and they are worried. Who will cook the turkey and make the pie? They don't want to eat fast food as their father threatens. Also they have tests. Tony has a party, their socks stink, nobody's making beds. The catch-and-release mousetrap my husband bought isn't working. They won't eat the cheese, Mom, Mickey told me. Try peanut butter, I suggested, and he hung up hooting wildly. Jelly too, Mom?

So I'm going home. I stopped packing my father's belongings, gave away only some of the clothes and unpacked the kitchen supplies. I've thrown sheets over the chairs, sofa, and bed to protect them from dust. I emptied the refrigerator. Jimmy Vusich offered to stop by every week to check on things through the winter, and yesterday I trudged across the woods to my father's neighbors to tell them I planned on keeping this property. They grinned with pleasure at my decision. "Hell of a guy," the man kept saying, while his wife disappeared into a pantry to bring me a jar of blueberry jam.

Even so, I don't want to leave. When I return, it will be another time, won't it? In these woods some creatures will have died and others migrated in. The ice might be gone and the shoreline slightly different. And I will be different as well and the sound of my father's voice just that much more distant.

The mail truck pulled into the driveway this morning just as I was putting my suitcase into the trunk. The postal carrier, a man named Steve Lamar, went to school with me and remembers that I helped him learn to read in second grade. He's shy and lanky and clearly likes saying hello to me, his eyes always more on the ground than on my face, as he hands me whatever loose ends of mail he has for my father. There is a mailbox up at the main road, but Steve has driven down every day since he learned I was here.

"So this is it, eh?" he asked today, seeing my packed car.

"The post office is supposed to forward the mail to me in Minneapolis for now," I explained, barely able to stand the look of disappointment on his face.

"Pretty nice out here though," he said. "Pretty nice place to live— or visit," he added.

"I know, Steve. I'll be back. Probably in spring."

"Oh sure. That's how it goes." He handed me a small stack of envelopes and bobbed his head up and down for no reason. "So," he said, "we'll see you then."

"Thank you, Steve. Thank you for bringing the mail down every day. It helped a lot in this cold weather."

I felt I should watch him turn the truck around and bump back up the road, then I came inside to look at the mail. Two of the envelopes contain junk and one is a bill for the telephone. But the last is a surprising brown envelope from New York with a written note and a typed sheet inside. The note, written in the same loopy script as the one I found days ago in my father's handkerchief drawer, says this:

Gigi —
Here's the gift I said I'd give you.
Maybe you are still well, as always.
And your Margaret too.
Corrine

And on the typed sheet I find this poem:

Spring and Fall: To a Young Child

Margaret, are you grieving
Over Goldengrove unleaving?
Leaves, like the things of man, you
With your fresh thoughts care for, can you?
Ah! as the heart grows older
It will come to such sights colder
By and by, nor spare a sigh
Though worlds of wanwood leafmeal lie;
And yet you will weep and know why.
Now no matter, child, the name:
Sorrow's springs are the same.
Nor mouth had, no nor mind, expressed
What heart heard of, ghost guessed:
It is the blight man was born for,
It is Margaret you mourn for.

—GERARD MANLEY HOPKINS

I read it again and again. It is fall, of course. And I do mourn.
Not just because my father has died, but because I am leaving his
small house empty for the long winter and because I married a
remote man and my sons are growing up and it is November no
matter where I go. This woman Corrine, she was a note hidden
under the fishing license and a reason my father wouldn't visit
New York with me. I believe she was the distraction that he kept
through all his years and, at the end, she sent this poem and little

else. Better my father is not here to read it over and over looking for words she never said and never would.

One winter when my father and I were on our own, before I had assembled any kind of teenage life apart from him, we went out to Dewey Lake—that was when Dewey was still working for him—and we drove down the boat launch, as we'd done before, and out onto the snowy ice in our two-tone Chevy Impala. I sat in the broad front seat setting cards all over in an attempt to beat myself at solitaire. My father was singing one of his blues favorites, doing both the words and the instrumentals, da da, da da da da, when the ice cracked under our weight. It shouldn't have, in midwinter, with a layer at least one foot thick over the dark water, but it had snowed the night before, hiding our view of the ice surface.

"Meggie, be still," my father said, as though my card mess could somehow sink us. He maneuvered the steering wheel, put the car in reverse and inched us back. I think we did not even breathe. We listened to the tires crunch on the snow, waiting for another crack in the ice that never came. Close to shore, my father gunned it and, once on solid ground, he stopped driving to collect himself.

"Wow, Dad," I remember saying. "Could we have drowned?"

He shook his head and kept shaking it. "That's the last time I drive out," he said finally. He rubbed my head. "That's it for us driving on the lake, Meggie."

"It worked before," I argued, but he didn't answer.

And now I hold this note and poem, a last gesture from the woman named Corrine. And he's gone. On Lost Lake, the winter's ice layer is forming. You see what I mean about all of this, the ventures out and away, the wide possibilities, the lost and never-ending loves. We have to pitch our chisels into the ice. Test the depth. And beware.